BEYOND *the* TEAM

OUT OF REACH BOOK FOUR

NEW YORK TIMES BESTSELLING AUTHOR
KAYLEE RYAN

Copyright © 2021 Kaylee Ryan

All Rights Reserved.
This book may not be reproduced in any manner whatsoever without the written permission of Kaylee Ryan, except for the use of brief quotations in articles and or reviews.

This book is a work of fiction. Names, characters, events, locations, businesses and plot are products of the author's imagination and meant to be used in a fictitious manner. Any resemblance to actual persons, living or dead, or actual events throughout the story are purely coincidental. The author acknowledges trademark owners and trademarked status of various products referenced in this work of fiction, which have been used without permission. The publication and use of these trademarks is not authorized, sponsored or associated by or with the trademark owners.
The following story contains sexual situations and strong language. It is intended for adult readers.

Cover Design: Perfect Pear Creative Covers
Cover Photography: Wander Aguair
Editing: Hot Tree Editing
Proofreading: Deaton Author Services & Editing 4 Indies
Formatting: Integrity Formatting

BEYOND *the* TEAM

OUT OF REACH BOOK FOUR

KAYLEE RYAN

CHAPTER 1

I DIDN'T THINK I'D BE here. After planning, organizing, and begging, I still didn't think my parents would go for it. Yes, I'm legally an adult, but I'm also the baby of three girls, and even though my older sisters weren't wild and crazy, my dad is still overprotective. Lucky for me, my middle sister, Parker, was coming to Florida to surprise her Major League boyfriend, Holden, and she helped me convince our parents, well, just Dad, really, to let me come with her. The time just happened to coincide with my spring break.

Luck is finally on my side.

My sister is off doing her thing, and I'm sitting here on the beach doing mine. In case you're wondering, my "thing" is absolutely nothing unless you want to count soaking up the Florida sun with my best friend, Karina.

This is only the second day of our five-day trip, and after the drama with Holden and Parker yesterday, it's good to relax and know that they're good. I talked to her last night and again this morning, and everything is all right with them. I stayed in Karina's room to give them some privacy. We have a two-bedroom suite, but nobody wants to hear them making out. Especially me.

"I love the beach," Karina says from her spot next to me.

"Me too, but I also love the mountains," I tell her. We both live in Tennessee, and while it's nice to escape to the ocean from time to time, the mountains will always be home to me.

"Too bad we can't have the best of both worlds," Karina muses.

"Yeah, but then we wouldn't have weeks like this." A visit to the beach to soak up the sun is definitely something to look forward to.

"Fair point." She laughs.

"Hey, did you decide if you're going to go through with parasailing?" I ask.

"Are you going to do it with me?"

"Nope."

"Come on, Peyton. Live a little."

"I'm not going to fly over shark-infested waters with nothing but a kite and some string holding me in the air."

"Chicken."

"I'll own that," I tell her. "My feet are perfectly fine being buried in the sand." My best friend is laughing her ass off, but that's okay with me. She's the crazy one who wants to feed herself to the sharks. She can laugh all she wants.

"Are you even going to get into the water while we're here?"

"I swam in the pool yesterday."

"I mean the ocean." She points at the waves that are crashing on the shore.

"We were in the water before we sat down."

"No. Our feet caught the waves on the shoreline. I mean, really go in, waist deep if not farther, and swim."

"I don't swim with fish," I remind her.

Before she can reply, a "Heads-up!" is called out, and the next thing I know, a Frisbee is landing at my feet. I go to reach for it, to give it back to the owner, but a shadow falls over me. I look up, up, and up to see the most gorgeous man I've ever laid eyes on. He has shaggy brown hair and a smile that rivals the Florida sun.

"Sorry about that," he says, reaching for the Frisbee.

"N-No problem," I stutter. Thankfully, we're outside in the sun, and he can't tell that the pink hue to my cheeks is from embarrassment and not the weather.

"I'm Griffin," he says, offering me his hand that's not holding the Frisbee.

"Peyton," I say, sliding my hand into his larger, rough, calloused one.

"Yo! Throw it back!" a male voice calls out.

"Allow me." Karina holds her hand out for the Frisbee, and Griffin hands it off without question.

I watch as she climbs to her feet and soars the Frisbee back to the group of guys that I'm assuming are Griffin's friends. "She's competitive."

"So are we." He grins, and the dimple in his cheek winks at me. "You wanna go for a swim?"

"Thank you, but I'm okay here. You can go back to your game." I smile at him to let him know I'm not being a bitch. At least, I hope I don't come off that way.

"Nah, looks like I've been replaced." He nods to where Karina has now joined his friends. He moves to stretch out on the corner of the blanket I'm lying on. He's on his side, facing me, his head propped up on his elbow. "So, Peyton, tell me about you."

"There's not much to know, really."

He reaches out and tucks a stray hair that the wind has loosened from my ponytail behind my ear. "I doubt that. Come on, give me something."

A swarm of butterflies releases in my belly when he turns that smile on me. "Fine, but you have to do the same."

"Deal."

"I'm here on spring break." I stop there and give him a pointed look.

"Come on now. You have to give me more than that."

"This is a group effort," I tease.

"I live here, but we're on spring break as well." He waits for me to offer more, but I'm tight-lipped. It's his turn to start. "I'm local to this area. I'm just a Florida resident coming to hang out at the beach for spring break."

"Nice. Karina and I both live in Tennessee. Nashville," I add.

"How long are you here?" he asks.

"Just five days. We're on day number two." I hold up two fingers and curse myself for being so awkward. I can't seem to help it. He's drop-dead gorgeous, and that smile keeps me from thinking straight.

He nods. "Well, it's a good thing our Frisbee crashed into you. There is no one better than a local to show you the sights. And by local, I mean me." He points at his chest. "Just in case you were wondering."

"So, let me get this straight. You want to spend your spring break showing me your hometown? That doesn't sound like the full college experience to me."

"Who says I'm in college?"

"You're on spring break."

He laughs. "Fine, you've got me there, but to answer your question, hell yes, I do."

"I don't want to abandon Karina." It's a lame excuse, but I

have to at least attempt to ward off his advances, right? I can't seem too eager.

"She can come too. Besides"—he glances over his shoulder—"it looks like she's already getting along with my friends."

I look down at my bikini-clad body and then back at Griffin. He, too, is looking at my bikini-clad body. My body heats, and I move my legs to ward off the desire that just a single look from him causes. "I'm going to need to change," I tell him.

His eyes pop to mine. "Or not." He grins.

"Let me talk to Karina." I move to stand, and he hops to his feet with catlike reflexes and throws his arm over my shoulders.

"Hey, fellas!" he calls out as we make our way across the sand to our friends. "How about some sightseeing with these lovely ladies?" He points at me with the hand that's not holding me to him and then at Karina.

"I'm in," Karina announces. Her wide eyes find mine. I know that look. She's surprised I'm standing here with Griffin's arm around my shoulders. I step out from his hold, and he lets me. I immediately miss his heat, but I stay where I am. I'm usually very reserved around guys because I never know if they're hitting on me because of my family or for me. I mean, come on. My dad was a major leaguer, my brother-in-law is a major leaguer, and my other sister is also dating a major leaguer. My family is pretty well known, which makes it hard for me to date.

"See..." Griffin leans down and whispers in my ear. Goose bumps break out across my skin from his hot breath against my face.

Unable to resist, I turn to look at him over my shoulder. "You sure you want to waste a day with two country girls?" I tease, trying to lighten the moment and not let on that my belly is flip-flopping at his nearness.

"Positive."

"Where are we headed first?" one of the guys asks.

"Lunch," Karina answers. "I'm starving."

"Seafood?" Griffin asks.

I shrug. "Not much of a seafood girl," I confess.

"That's because they don't do seafood in Tennessee like they do in Florida." He winks. "Besides, if you hate it, you can always order chicken." The laughter behind his eyes makes him even that more attractive. He seems like a good time, and I can't help but want to get to know him better.

"I'm trusting you." I point my index finger at him.

He grabs my hand and brings it to his lips. "I've got you, Peyton," he says, placing a kiss on the palm of my hand.

"Smooth talker."

He shrugs. "I prefer charming."

"Oh, you're charming, all right." I laugh. He once again places his arm over my shoulders, and this time, I don't move away. I have a feeling he'd just keep doing it, and then there's that little tiny morsel of me that really likes it.

Ten minutes later, Karina and I are standing outside of a taco truck with Griffin and three of his friends. "This?" I turn to look at him. "A taco truck?"

"Ah," he says, tapping me on the nose. "This isn't a normal taco truck. We've got fish tacos and crab tacos to choose from. You, my friend, are going to try both."

I cross my arms over my chest in defiance. "I thought you said that if I didn't like it, I could order chicken?" I ask, calling him out.

He grips my shoulders and walks me to the edge of the truck. Sure enough, sitting behind the taco truck is yet another truck. This one is called The Chicken Queen, and there's a big picture of a basket of tenders and fries on the side. "Like I said, I've got you." He grins.

"I'll grab me something," I say, taking a step toward the chicken truck.

"Not so fast, little lady," he teases.

"I'm not little." His calling me lady reminds me of my dad, and I don't want to think about him now.

He stands to his full height, well over six feet. "You are to me."

He's not wrong. He's almost a head taller than I am. "I'm going to grab some food," I say, taking another step toward the chicken truck.

Griffin wraps his arms around me from behind and lifts me into the air. My breathing grows erratic from being this close to him. "Tacos first," he says, his lips next to my ear. He carries me with ease to the window of the taco truck before placing me on my feet.

"I don't even know what to order," I say, trying not to pout and make myself look like a fool in front of him. I'm not the most adventurous person in the world when it comes to food.

"I'll take care of you," he says, his voice husky.

I know he's talking about food, but my mind drifts to other ways he could take care of me. One would be the ache he's caused between my thighs. "Let's do this, so I can order my chicken," I tell him. I've never reacted this way to a guy before. My body never betrays me. I don't seem to have a choice when it comes to Griffin.

He throws his head back in laughter, and I turn to watch him. "I promise you that if you don't like them, I'll buy you a basket of chicken tenders."

"Deal." I nod. He steps up to the window and rattles off an order that seems to be way too much food for two people, but what do I know? "That's a lot of food for two people," I voice my thoughts.

"I made sure there was enough for Karina too."

His words have me feeling all warm and gooey inside, and it has nothing to do with the heat of the sun. "Thank you."

"You're welcome."

"My turn," one of the guys says, stepping up to the window.

"Are you eating here?" Karina asks.

"I told this one"—I point at Griffin—"that I would try it. We have a deal. If I hate it, he buys me chicken from the next truck."

"Don't worry," he chimes in. "I'm confident. I ordered enough for all three of us."

"Wow. Thanks. I've never tried it, but I'm game," Karina tells him.

"See, Peyton, where is your sense of adventure?" he teases.

"This one is a picky eater," Karina announces.

I shrug. "I'm not going to deny it."

"Well, growing up, my mom always told me that I couldn't claim that I didn't like something if I'd never tried it, so today, you are going to step out of your food bubble and open your horizons."

"You've got your work cut out for you." Karina laughs.

Griffin's eyes hold mine. "I think I'm up for the challenge."

I'm sure I'm way off base, but something in his gaze tells me he's talking about more than just the mountain of food he just ordered.

"You're going to love it," his friend, who's taller than him and has white-blond hair, assures me.

"Thanks..." I let the words trail off.

"Right, proper introductions." Griffin throws his arm over my shoulders once more. "This is Peyton, and that's Karina." He points at where she's standing on my other side. "This is Sam." He gestures to the tall white-haired guy. "This is Daniel." He points at the smallest of the group, who also seems to be bulkier than the others. He reminds me of a football player. "And this is Oliver." Griffin nods toward his last friend. This one is the same height as Griffin and the same build, but he has jet-black hair.

"Nice to meet you," Karina and I say at the same time, making everyone laugh.

"Are you sisters?" Sam asks.

"No. Best friends since kindergarten," Karina answers.

"I have two older sisters," I say without thinking. I usually try to keep my family to myself. Karina turns to look at me and raises her eyebrows. I pretend not to notice.

"What about you?" Oliver asks Karina.

"Only child."

"Anthony!" the server from the food truck calls out.

"That's us." Griffin grins. "Go find us a picnic table. I'll be right there."

"Can you carry all of that?" I ask.

"Woman, you wound me." He places his hand over his heart. "I've got this. The guys can help. Go sit."

Karina links her arm through mine, and we set off to find a picnic table on this section of the beach. "He's hot. Hell, they're all hot," she whispers.

"Right?"

"He's into you."

"Who?" I pretend not to know because it's unreal to me, the connection I feel so soon.

"Griffin, that's who."

"He's just being nice," I defend.

"Uh-huh." She chuckles. "We'll see about that. We have the rest of today and three more days."

"He lives here. I live in Tennessee. It would never work."

She pulls her phone out of her bag and taps the screen, holding it up. "Repeat that," she says.

"What?"

"I want evidence, so when I say I told you so, I have proof."

"Stop." I push her hand away.

"What are we filming?" Griffin asks. He sets a huge brown bag and three bottles of water on the table.

"Oh, I was just telling Peyton here that you two seem to be hitting it off. I wanted to record the moment that she denied it."

I glare at my soon-to-be-former best friend. "She's just messing with you."

"Hit record," Griffin says.

"Action." Karina grins.

"I, Griffin Anthony, want to go on record stating that Peyton—whose last name I don't know yet—and I are most definitely hitting it off." He winks at the camera.

"Saved to the archives," Karina says. Her voice is giddy.

"What are we waiting on? Let's eat," Daniel says as he, Sam, and Oliver join us on the opposite side of the picnic table.

"All right." Griffin begins to remove items from his brown bag. "There is a fish and a crab taco for each of you," he says, passing them to us.

I unwrap the first one. "Which one is this?" I ask.

He leans over, getting all up in my personal space, which I don't mind at all. "That's the fish."

Karina is the first to take a bite. "Wow," she says, covering her mouth with her hand. "That's so good," she mumbles.

"Your turn." Griffin leans his shoulder into mine.

Lifting it to my lips, I see that all eyes are on me. "You all can eat," I tell his friends.

"Nope. We need to witness the full experience like we did with Karina." Oliver points at my best friend, who is taking another big bite of her fish taco.

"Fine." Lifting my taco, I take a small bite, and the taste explodes on my tongue. "Good," I say after swallowing.

"Told you," Griffin boasts.

We make small talk while we eat, and before I know it, I'm opening up my crab taco. Karina goes first with all of us watching. Her eyes literally roll back in her head.

"That's better than sex," she announces.

"Hey now, that's a little extreme," Sam says, serious as a heart attack.

"You're up," Oliver tells me.

I repeat the process, starting with a small bite, and Karina is right. This one is better than the other. "Wow," I say once I've finished. "That's so good."

Griffin leans in close, his lips next to my ear. "I've got you," he says huskily.

The funny thing is, he's right. And it's not just because he didn't steer me wrong as far as lunch goes. He's got my attention, something very few before him have managed to do. I don't trust guys easily. Maybe it's because we're so far away from home and he doesn't know my family. And maybe, just maybe, it's him.

CHAPTER 2
Griffin

W E'VE SPENT THE ENTIRE DAY at the beach. Peyton and Karina have been with us the majority of the day, and I can't say I'm mad about it. They're both beautiful girl-next-door types. However, Peyton—with her long brown hair, those curves, and that smile—is the one who's captured my attention.

They're both the kinds of girls you take home to meet your parents. I can't help but smile when I think about bringing her home to meet my family. Mom would love her. She'd also probably pass out from shock, considering I've never brought anyone home.

Oliver and I were best friends growing up, and even in high school, we never saddled ourselves with dates for the dances like homecoming and prom. There were way too many beautiful girls to dance with to commit to just one. Baseball was a big deal at our school. Hell, all sports were a big deal at our school, and we rode the high of the status being on the team brought us. Of course, it helped that we both dominated on the field.

Now, here we are, freshmen in college and living by the same philosophies. Baseball is life, and going pro is what we both want. Daniel and Sam enjoy it, but going pro isn't their endgame. Oliver and I have laser focus when it comes to making our dreams of playing in the major leagues come true.

"I'm starving," Sam announces.

"Yeah, it's late. We should be getting back to the hotel," Karina adds.

"Where are you staying?" I ask her.

She points over her shoulder to the Casa Playa Resort. "There."

"Why don't we grab some dinner, and then we'll walk you back?" I suggest, my eyes moving back and forth between Peyton and Karina. I'm really not ready for the night to end.

"Thank you, but we promised Karina's parents that we would have dinner with them when we got back," Peyton answers.

"You're on spring break with your parents?" Sam asks, horrified.

Karina laughs. "Yeah, but it's not as bad as it sounds. They're not insisting we spend every waking moment with them."

"And you just happened to tag along?" Daniel asks Peyton.

"Kind of. My older sister is a senior in college, and she's here with her boyfriend," Peyton explains.

"So it's a family affair." Oliver nods. "I like it."

"What are you doing after?" I sound desperate, even to my own ears, and maybe I am.

Peyton glances over at Karina, and she shrugs. "Nothing that I'm aware of."

"Meet us out here." I point at where we're standing.

"Put the guy out of his misery," Sam chimes in.

Peyton smiles. "Yeah, we'll meet you back here."

"Maybe you should give him your number," Daniel tells her. "You know, in case you're running late or whatever." He smirks.

"Communication is important. In fact, Karina, you should probably give me yours, you know, just in case my boy Griff's is dead or lost or something," Oliver adds. He's not even trying to hide his grin.

"Wow, you four stick together, huh?" Peyton asks.

"Wingman," Daniel, Sam, Oliver, and I all say at the same time, making the girls laugh.

"How about you give us your numbers, and when we're done, we'll text you?" Karina counters.

"Playing hard to get, I see." Sam winks at her.

"You already know where we're staying, which is too much. We're two women, and you're four men. We're easily outnumbered here. I think the safest bet is for us to have your numbers. Or not." Karina shrugs.

"Hey, now, let's not talk like that." Daniel holds his hands up. "We'll gladly give you beautiful ladies our digits."

Karina pulls out her phone and begins to take the guys' numbers down. When she turns to look at me, I nod toward Peyton. "You ready?" I ask her.

"For what?"

"My number."

A slow smile crosses her face as she reaches into her bag and pulls out her phone. I rattle off my number and watch as she enters it into her phone before dropping her phone back into her bag.

"Well, boys, it's been real," Karina says, linking her arm with Peyton's.

"Boys?" Sam scoffs with no heat.

Karina grins. "Well, you've yet to prove otherwise." She waves, and together they turn and head toward their hotel.

I stand there and watch them leave. I don't take my eyes off them until they disappear into the hotel. The silence from my friends tells me they're doing the same thing.

"Damn," Daniel says. "Anyone calling dibs?" he asks.

"Peyton," I say automatically.

"Yeah, we thought so." Oliver chuckles. "The friend?"

Daniel raises his hand, and I toss my head back in laughter. "I mean, I'm just looking for some fun, and she seems all kinds of fun."

Oliver grumbles something under his breath, but I'm too caught up in Peyton's gaze to try to decipher what it was.

"Food. I need food before my stomach starts to eat itself," Sam declares.

"You're always hungry. Where do you put it?" I ask him.

"Hey, it takes calories for all of this," he says, rubbing his hands over his six-pack.

"Well, I don't know about you all, but I'm thinking we eat in the restaurant." Daniel points at the hotel the girls just disappeared into.

I slap him on the shoulder. "You, my man, are a genius." I know he's into Karina, and I've already made it clear I'm into Peyton. Sam doesn't care. He just wants to eat, and Oliver, well, I'm not exactly sure what's up with him, but he's in. Without another word, the four of us make our way to the lobby of Casa Playa and to their in-house restaurant.

Our food has long since been demolished, yet we're still sitting here at this table right next to the restaurant entrance, shooting the shit, hoping to either hear from or see the girls. Daniel flirted with the hostess to score us this seat. I made sure to give him a high five as soon as she walked away. However, there hasn't been a single sighting or message from either of them.

"Is your phone not dead yet? You've only checked it a million times since we sat down," Oliver goads me.

"Fuck off." I laugh. I know my best friend wants to say more, but he doesn't. I'm surprised because he's usually calling me out on my shit.

"Guys, we've been here for two hours. I think it's safe to say we're not going to run into them here. We should probably go and let the server have this table," Sam comments. "My sister is a server, and she hates it when people just hang around. Most of the time, they leave a shit tip."

"Well, this place adds the tip to the bill, but we can leave some extra cash," I assure him. The four of us reach for our wallets. Our bills were already paid. Each of us drops some additional cash on the table before we leave the restaurant.

"Now what?" Oliver asks.

"You know, I'm pretty sure stalking is illegal," a female voice says from behind us where we're standing in the lobby trying to decide where to go next.

All four of us turn to face the voice, and I can't help but smile when I see Peyton and Karina standing there smiling. Peyton's hair is pulled up in a ponytail, and she's changed into a white sundress that makes her tits look incredible. Who am I kidding? They looked incredible earlier too.

My feet propel me forward, and I take her hand in mine before leaning in to kiss her cheek. "I missed you," I tell her. I stand back to my full height and smile down at her. I don't know what's gotten into me. I'm not an asshole to girls, but I've never told one that I missed her. Especially not after only knowing them a handful of hours.

Her cheeks turn the lightest shade of pink, and my dick twitches. "How was dinner?" I ask, forcing myself to take a step back.

"Good. My sister and her boyfriend joined us, so it was a family affair," Peyton replies.

"All right, ladies, what are we getting into tonight?" Sam claps his hands and rubs them together with a mischievous glint in his eye.

I want to tell him that Peyton and I are going to walk on the beach and they could do their own thing, but that's a bit much even for me. It's not even that I want to fuck her. I mean, I do, I really *really* do, but that's not it. She's just genuine and down to earth, and after a campus full of cleat chasers hoping to latch onto one of us who are destined to make it to the majors, she's a breath of fresh air.

"You're the locals." Karina laughs. "You tell us."

"Some friends of ours are building a fire down on the beach. We could go hang out there," Daniel suggests.

"Wait, aren't fires illegal on the beach?" Peyton asks.

"Technically, yes, but as long as it's small, and we clean up, they never say anything to us. The officers who patrol are pretty relaxed on that law, really," I explain.

"Besides, it's at the corner end of the beach. As long as we don't cause havoc, we're good," Sam adds.

Peyton looks up at me. "Are you sure we're not going to get arrested?"

"I'm sure." I nod.

She glances over at Karina. "What do you think?"

"Will there be alcohol?" Karina asks.

"Oh no, you don't," Peyton warns her. "I took care of you the last time, and I'm not dragging drunk you into your shared suite with your parents, and you know Parker won't be thrilled about me dragging you into ours either."

"I'll take it slow, and Parker loves me." Karina sticks her tongue out at Peyton.

"She does love you, and so do I, but that doesn't mean I want to drag your drunk ass back to the hotel."

"Who is Parker? Where is Parker, and if Parker is a she, is she hot?" Sam asks.

Peyton grins. "Parker is my sister. She's beautiful, and she's taken."

"Are you sure? I mean, she's passing up all of this," Sam says, lifting his shirt.

Karina and Peyton share a look, one I can't decipher before they both turn to Sam. "We're sure," they say at the same time.

"Wow, that's some freaky shit. How long did you say the two of you have been friends?" Oliver asks.

"Kindergarten," they both answer.

"I promise to get you both back to the hotel safely," I speak up.

"No offense, I appreciate the offer, but we don't really know you. Trusting you when we're inebriated isn't the wisest move," Peyton answers.

"My boy here is a standup dude," Sam offers.

"I'm sure he is." Peyton smiles. "However, I stand behind the fact that we don't know any of you, so while I appreciate the offer, we won't need you."

"Damn," Oliver mutters. "I like this one."

"Come on, ladies." Daniel links one arm through Peyton's and the other through Karina's. "The bonfire awaits." He leads them away from our little group with a smirk on his lips.

"You going to let him move in on your girl like that?" Oliver asks me.

"She's not my girl."

"This is going to be fun," he says, clamping a hand down on my shoulder.

"We already know they're fun," I counter, as we begin to follow Daniel and now Sam, who has caught up to them.

"Not the girls, I mean you."

"What in the hell are you talking about?"

"I'm talking about watching you fall for this girl."

"Whoa, hold up. No one said anything about falling for anyone," I correct him.

"You keep telling yourself that, my man." Oliver grins.

"You've lost your damn mind. She doesn't even live here. If I decided to start a relationship, it wouldn't be with a girl who lives states away."

"You sure about that?" he questions me.

"I'm positive. They're cool, and she's fun to hang around."

"You called dibs."

"Yeah, to keep you jokers from making a move."

"Uh-huh, we'll go with that," he says with a chuckle.

"Come on, slowpokes!" Sam calls back to us.

Oliver and I lift a hand, letting him know we heard him and we're making our way there. We walk in silence for a few minutes until Oliver speaks up again. "You know it's fine, right?"

"What's fine?"

"To fall for her?"

"Stop." I groan, dropping my head back. "I'm not falling for anyone. I'm keeping my eye on the prize, on my goal. We have an endgame. I haven't forgotten that."

"I hear you," he says.

I can tell by his tone that he doesn't believe me. It's not that I don't want to find someone. I grew up watching my parents, and I don't think any two people are more in love than they are. However, the career I want is not for everyone. And even though I'm a freshman, scouts came to watch us play in high school. Oliver and I are both on the radar for the pros. Word travels fast, and it's hard to know who's interested in you for you and who wants you as their meal ticket. Peyton seems easygoing, but I barely know the girl.

It's way too soon to be talking about falling, and long-distance relationships, and all that. She's nice, and I want to hang out with her while she's here. Maybe we'll keep in touch? But I'm certain that's as far as it's going to go.

When we finally catch up to them, Daniel and Sam are making introductions. I see my buddies and their interest, and well, like I said, I like her, and she doesn't need to be used like that. I walk up next to her and slide my arm around her shoulders.

"Wanna take a walk?"

"Where to?"

"Just down by the water." I point at the shoreline about fifty or so feet away.

"Hey." Peyton places her arm on Karina's. "We're going to walk down to the water," she tells her friend. "Will you be okay?"

"I'll make sure of it," Oliver speaks up.

I'm not sure what it is with him today, but I'm grateful. "He's good people. I promise."

"Stranger, remember?" Peyton reminds me.

"Hold up." Karina pulls her phone out of her back pocket and takes a picture of us, and then Daniel, Sam, and Oliver. "You know, just in case." She shrugs.

"You'll be able to see us the entire time," I promise, which seems to appease her. "Ready?" I ask Peyton.

"Sure," she agrees.

I hold my hand out for her, and she takes it. I don't hold hands with girls, so I'm not sure what made me do it, but I don't hate it. I kind of like the softness of her fingers entwined with mine.

"I love the ocean," she says. It's the dark of night, so you can't really see much, but the moon is bright, the stars are shining, and the sound of the waves lets you know it's there.

"You ever thought of moving?"

"I love the mountains too," she admits. "And Tennessee is my home. It's where my family is. I couldn't imagine moving away from them. What about you? You plan on staying in Florida?"

"I'm not sure. I'm hoping to go pro, and then I won't really have much of a say as to where I'm living."

"Ah, an athlete. What sport?"

"Baseball."

"Good game. I play softball. In fact, our season starts the day we get back to campus."

"Are you any good?" I ask her.

"I can hold my own. What about you? Is going pro a real possibility?"

"Yeah, that's what my coach tells me. Recruiters are hanging around already, and I had scouts at most of my games in high school."

"You're a freshman, right?" she asks.

"Yeah, you?"

"Yep." She looks out over the ocean. "I hope all your dreams come true, Griffin."

I step behind her and wrap my arms around her. She doesn't even flinch when I do it. Instead, she rests her hands over mine that lock around her waist. She leans back against my chest, and a small sigh escapes her lips.

It's out of character for me, but something in her tone tells me that she's being sincere, and that touches something inside me I didn't even know existed. A part of me is drawn to her, and I can't explain why.

"Thank you," I say, my lips next to her ear. I don't kiss her like I want to. Instead, I hold her while we stare out at the darkened waters, shimmering in the moonlight.

CHAPTER 3
Peyton

"I CAN FEEL YOU STARING at me," I grumble into my pillow. It was late by the time the guys walked us back to the hotel last night, so Karina crashed in my room with me. Thankfully, Parker and I have a two-bedroom suite. I don't need to see her and Holden all tangled up in bed together, and by the two pairs of shoes sitting next to the wall when I kicked mine off, I know he's here with her. Of course, he is. He's head over heels in love with my sister. Where else would he be?

"That's because your phone keeps going off," Karina fires back.

"Who in the hell is texting me at this hour?"

She laughs. "It's after nine, sleepyhead. Did all that cuddling with Griffin last night take it out of you?" she asks, her voice sugary sweet.

"Stop." I swat at her arm. "Besides, you and Daniel looked pretty close too."

"We were flirting."

"So were we," I defend.

"Nah, what you had going on was altogether different."

I peel open my eyes and look at her. "How do you figure?"

"I don't really know. The best way I can explain it is that it looked like the two of you were together. Like you had been together for a long time. You move, he moves. He moves, you move. It was really something to see."

I should tell her that she's crazy, but then I'd be lying. That's exactly how it felt to be with Griffin last night. "He didn't make a move," I confess.

"Yeah, it didn't look like that to me. I mean, it didn't look like he was just trying to get his dick wet. It was weird, Peyton. I've never seen two people just... connect like that."

"You want to know something even weirder?" I ask her.

"What's that?"

"Feeling it," I say as my phone vibrates again. Reaching over on the nightstand, I grab it and swipe at the screen. I have several text messages from Griffin and one from Oliver.

Griffin:

Morning, beautiful.

That one was sent two hours ago. They just kept coming at random from then until now.

Do I get to see you today?

How about breakfast?

Peyton?

Oliver:

> Girl, you've got my boy
> all tied up in knots. Can
> you put us all out of our
> misery and reply to
> him? Even if it's to blow
> him off.

I laugh at that one. "Who is it?" Karina asks.

"Griffin, and then one from Oliver." I hand her my phone, so she can read the messages.

"Damn, girl, that must have been some stellar snuggling." She laughs.

"Stop." I take my phone back from her and reply to Oliver first. I can't have Griffin thinking I'm falling at his feet, even though I kind of am. There is just something about him.

> Just woke up. Ever
> heard of sleeping in?

Oliver:

> She's alive.

> Your boy is waiting
> for his reply.

His message is followed by a string of laughing emojis and a picture of Griffin sitting on the couch, staring down at his phone. I show my screen to Karina, and she laughs. Pulling my phone back, I type out a reply to Griffin.

> Just woke up. Do
> you not sleep in?

Griffin:

> Not last night

> **Everything okay?**

Griffin:
> I'm not sure.

I don't know him well enough to pry. I bite down on my bottom lip, trying to think of what to say, but his next message comes in before I can.

Griffin:
> I couldn't stop thinking about you.

> That's not me.

> What are you doing to me?

Butterflies take flight in my belly. I want to tell him I thought about him too. I stayed up way later than I should have, which is why I slept in this morning. However, before I can contemplate my reply, I get another message. This one is from Oliver.

Oliver:
> What kind of spell did you cast on my best friend?

It's followed by a picture of Griffin sitting on the same couch. Only there is a sexy grin pulling at his lips as he smiles down at his phone.

> **Are you calling me a witch?**

Oliver:
> No. But you are responsible for that goofy ass grin.

I'm now wearing a goofy-ass grin of my own.

I'm not sure you're right, but I'll take the credit.

I close out of his message, switch back to Griffin's, and type out a reply.

If it makes you feel any better, I thought about you too. I'd say we're even.

Griffin:

Can I see you today?

What did you have in mind?

My phone rings, and I drop it as I'm fumbling to answer the call. Karina laughs and picks it up from the bed between us and hands it to me. "Hello," I say in a rush.

"Peyton," Griffin greets. "Come to my place today. We can swim and just hang out." He expels a breath as if he'd been waiting hours to invite us over.

"Your place?" I look at Karina with wide eyes, and she nods, pointing at her chest.

"Yeah. I can swing by and pick you and Karina up." I love that he included my best friend without me having to ask.

"I'm not sure what we're getting into today," I tell him. "I'll talk to Karina and let you know."

"I'm in," Karina calls out, moving to practically lay on top of me. "Whatever it is, Griffin, we're in," she says again with a mischievous glint in her eye.

Griffin's deep laughter fills my ears. "Tell me what time to be there, Peyton."

"Give us a couple of hours? I want to talk to my sister for a bit, and we both need showers." That doesn't sound too desperate. I do want to check in with Parker, but I don't need to. I just want to make sure things are still solid with her and Holden. I'm sure they are, but I'd still feel better checking in with her.

"I'll be there at noon. You wanna give me your room number so I can pick you up properly?" Griffin asks.

"Is this a date?" I counter.

"It's whatever you want it to be, Peyton." His reply is soft, almost as if he's uncertain.

"That's not what I asked you, Griffin."

"I want it to be," he admits.

I'm smiling so big I can feel my cheeks stretch. "We'll meet you in the lobby."

He chuckles. "I can live with that. I'll see you soon, Peyton."

"See you soon."

"Oh, and Peyton," he adds quickly, which has me pulling the phone back to my ear.

"Yeah?"

"This is most definitely a date." With that, the line goes dead.

"You're blushing," Karina states the obvious. I can feel the heat in my cheeks.

"He says it's a date. He wants us to come to his place and swim. The guys will be there."

"See." Karina sits up and points at me. "I told you. There is something there. It's been fun to watch."

"We spent one day with him and his friends."

"One day, the entire day, and the connection was instant. We can all see it. Hell, even Oliver sees it."

"He's just being a good wingman." I'm not sure if I'm trying to convince her or myself.

"Come on, Peyton. You know better," she scolds.

"Fine. I'll admit there's a connection, but that's all it is. He lives here. I live in Tennessee. It could never work."

"Never say never, my friend." She tosses off the covers and climbs out of bed. "I'm going to run to my room, check in with the parental units, and shower. I'll be back here by noon so that we can go to the lobby together."

"Sounds like a plan."

"Aren't you glad we went shopping for those new bathing suits you said we didn't need for this trip?" she asks as she makes her way to the door.

"Thank you for insisting I purchase five new pieces of swimwear," I reply sarcastically.

"You're welcome," she singsongs her way out the door.

Pulling myself out of bed, I pick out my clothes for the day, trying hard not to think about Griffin as I do, and head to the shower.

Thirty minutes later, I'm walking into the living area of the suite to find my sister on the couch, holding her e-reader. "Good morning," I say, taking a seat next to her.

"Hey, where's Karina?"

"She left to shower and get ready. We met a few people yesterday, and we're going to spend the day by the pool with them."

"People? Are any of them hot?" she asks.

"They all are," I admit.

"Which one has your eye?"

"Griffin." I sigh.

"Aw, I like you like this," she says. "I've never seen you let yourself fall. You have stars in your eyes, little sister," she teases.

"Stop it." I laugh. "I do not have stars in my eyes. He's nice and definitely easy on the eyes. He doesn't know me as a Monroe. He just knows me as Peyton. I don't get that back home."

Parker nods. "Yeah, I get that. So, what are your plans today?" she asks.

"Griffin and his friends invited us to hang out at his place at the pool."

"Be careful, Peyton. You don't know this guy."

"I know. My gut tells me that I can trust him."

"Can you get me an address of where you're going to be?" she asks. "I'm not trying to be all over-the-top protective big sister, but you're young and beautiful, and it's spring break, and I've heard horror stories."

"No, I get it. Let me text him and ask for his address." Reaching for my phone that I set on the couch cushion beside me, I fire off a text.

> Hey, sorry to ask this, but can you send me your address? Or the address of where we're going to be today?

Griffin:

> You have nothing to be sorry for. That's smart on your part.

> Well, that all goes to Parker.

Griffin:

> Middle sister, right?

> So, he listens.

Griffin:

> It's hard not to when it's you who's speaking.

His text is followed by another with a picture of his license, and then his actual address that matches his license typed out.

I turn my phone to show it to Parker, and she laughs. "Okay, I admit he's charming," she says as my phone alerts me to another message. She snatches my phone and reads it, and nods her approval. She hands it back to me, wearing a smirk.

Griffin:

If you'd let me come to your room to pick you up, I could meet her.

"He can come up here," Parker tells me.

"I didn't want to risk Holden being here."

"He's at training camp all day."

"I'll stay here with you. I can cancel."

"Not a chance. Autumn and I are planning to do some shopping and hit the beach for a little bit of sun."

"Are you sure?" I ask just as my phone rings. I turn it so she can see that it's Griffin calling.

"Answer it."

I roll my eyes and swipe at the screen. "Hello?"

"Let me come to your room."

"It's a hotel, Griffin. It's not like you need to come to the door to meet my parents."

"No, but your big sister is here, and that's the next best thing."

"That's really not necessary. I'll meet you in the lobby at noon."

"Fine. I'm sitting on the bench next to the elevators."

"What?"

"I'm sitting—" he starts, but I stop him.

"I heard you. Why are you here? We don't meet for another hour or so?"

"Because I was driving Oliver crazy, and I thought if you changed your mind and wanted me to pick you up properly for our date, I'd be close."

"So, you're what? Going to just sit downstairs by the elevator until noon?"

"That was the plan."

"You're crazy." I laugh.

"About you."

"You barely know me," I counter. I look over at Parker, and I can't decipher the look on her face, but it's obvious she's listening intently to our conversation.

"Yeah," he agrees. "It sounds insane, even to me, but here I am." He chuckles.

"Tell him to come up," Parker says loud enough that she knows Griffin will hear her.

"I heard that," he says, confirming what I already knew.

"5602."

"Thank fuck," he mutters. "I'm on my way," he says. I hear the elevator doors whoosh open.

"Okay."

"See you soon," he says and ends the call.

"Wow. You've got it bad." Parker laughs.

"I don't know him."

"That doesn't mean you can't be vibing on the guy."

"Vibing? Really Parker?"

"What?" She laughs. "Fine, crushing, is that better?"

"Can you crush on someone you just met?"

"Yep."

I don't get to answer before there's a knock on our door. Standing, I wipe my sweaty palms on my jean shorts and make my way to the door. When I open it, I'm surprised to find Holden and not Griffin.

"Holden? Come on in." I step back, and then panic hits me. Griffin is on his way up, and he's going to see Holden, and that's going to ruin it all. How am I going to know that he's here for me and not my connections to baseball?

"Hey, Peyton." Holden leans in and kisses my cheek as he passes me and rushes to my sister.

I look over my shoulder and watch as she stands to greet him, and he lifts her into his arms and kisses her like it's been weeks since he's seen her and not hours. "What are you doing here?" I hear her ask, but I don't hear what he says because there's a tapping on my shoulder.

I turn to find Griffin smiling down at me. "You look beautiful," he says, pulling me into a hug.

His scent, so much like the ocean, wraps around me, and I don't know how but it's comforting to me. I've known him for just over twenty-four hours. How is that possible?

"Let him in," Parker calls out.

"You don't have to do this," I tell him. I'm not ready to lose him even though I just found him.

"Come on, Peyton. It's going to be fine. I promise." He presses his lips to my temple, entwines his hand with mine, and leads me into the room.

"Parker, Holden, this is Griffin."

"Parker, it's nice to meet you." Griffin offers his hand that's not holding mine to my sister to shake. Once she does, he then looks at Holden. "Holden, nice to meet you," he says again, offering his hand to Holden. I watch him closely for recognition, but his expression doesn't change.

"You too," Holden says, shaking his hand. "How long have you known our Peyton?" Holden asks, and I have to fight not to roll my eyes.

Griffin gives my hand a gentle squeeze and smiles down at me. "We met yesterday."

"Right, so we're going to go," I say, tugging on his hand.

"Hold up," Holden calls out. "You can't expect me to let you just leave with this guy. You barely know him."

I look over at my sister and give her a pleading look, but she just smiles and shrugs.

"I have a picture of his driver's license. I can send it to you," I tell Holden.

Before he can reply, there's a knock on the door. Holden walks to the door and pulls it open. "Come in. Peyton has a guy here."

"Who is he?" I hear the newcomer ask, and groan when I recognize the voice as Cameron, my brother-in-law.

"Parker," I hiss.

"What? He stopped to see me. They had a quick break, and Cam wanted to switch out his cleats and left them in his room. I didn't know," she replies.

Hot tears prick my eyes. It's ridiculous that I'm upset, but I really like Griffin. I just wanted him for me. Just this once, I wanted to be Peyton. Not Peyton Monroe.

"Hi, I'm Griffin," he announces to Cameron, offering him his hand that again is not holding mine. I try to step away from him, but he tightens his hold and turns to me. "What's wrong?" He must see it in my eyes because his hands cradle my cheeks instantly, and he bends so that we're eye to eye. "What is it?"

"Nothing. I'm fine. Let's just go."

"We can't let you just leave with him," Cameron says. His reply is much like Holden's.

"You're not my father. Either of you. I'm an adult. I can do what I want."

"You're our sister," they both reply at the same time, making me groan, and my heart melts with love for the two of them at the same time. I'm a mess.

"What can I do?" Griffin asks.

"Get me out of here." I know the chances of him defying two Major League baseball players is slim to none, but I find myself hoping he takes me seriously.

Griffin presses his lips to my forehead, slides his arm around my waist, and faces my family. "I'll gladly send you my address of where we're going to be. I promise you that I won't let anything happen to her, and I will personally deliver her to this room when she's ready to come home."

His words have the tears threatening to fall. I didn't expect his reply. Who am I kidding? I didn't expect him either, but here we are.

"Do you know who we are?" Cameron asks, crossing his muscled arms over his chest.

"Yes."

"So you know we have connections?" Holden adds.

Great, here we go. "Guys, just stop. We're leaving," I say, pulling on Griffin's hand.

"You won't need them," Griffin says, his voice firm.

"You make sure that we won't," Cameron replies.

"Okay, boys, that's enough. Obviously, you're not scaring him, but I think you're going to cause Peyton to lose her shit. Let them go." Parker steps toward me and wraps me in a hug. "Be safe, little sister. I love you."

"Love you too," I tell her, hugging her back with one arm because Griffin refuses to release my hand.

"Now," she says, stepping back, "I would appreciate it if you would send me his address. Just in case."

"Send her my license," Griffin chimes in.

"You all are aware how ridiculous this is, right?" I ask, rolling my eyes.

"Just keeping you safe, Peyton," Holden says gently.

"What's the point of having big brothers if we can't give your dates shit?" Cameron asks.

"By marriage," I counter. And then I turn to Holden. "And you're not even married yet."

Holden turns to Parker. "We need to do something about that," he tells her, and she smiles.

"I love you, all three of you, but we're leaving. I'll text you where I am."

"Be safe," Parker calls out.

This time, Griffin lets me drag him out of the room. As soon as the door shuts behind us, he's pulling me into his embrace.

"I don't know what that was, but I'm sorry if I caused problems with your family. I just wanted to do this right."

"You didn't. I just… never mind. Can we go?"

"We're going to have to talk about this," he says, leading me toward the elevator.

"Why?"

"Because it obviously upset you."

"It's not your job to take care of me."

"Yeah," he agrees. "But what if I want it to be?"

"You barely know me."

"I want to know everything about you, Peyton."

"We're early. Karina's probably not ready yet."

"That's fine. Let's take a walk around the grounds."

I lace my fingers with his and let him lead me outside. I get lost in my thoughts, and he lets me. It didn't seem to faze him at all that Cameron and Holden were in my suite. I don't know what to think about that. Is he pretending? Does he really not care? I guess only time will tell.

CHAPTER 4
Griffin

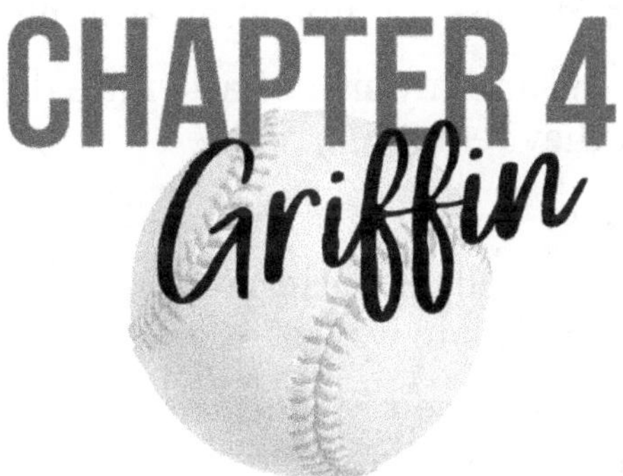

H OLY FUCK. MY HAND GRIPS Peyton's tightly as we walk around the hotel. It's a small path that I've seen many guests use to run on. Today, it's serving as a route for a leisurely stroll with a beautiful girl.

A beautiful girl who is so deeply connected to the game that I love... and I'm not sure how to process it. Cameron Taylor and Holden Bailey are her family. From what I gather, one is married to a sister, and the other is about to be?

I can't believe I was just standing there with two of the greats, and I basically told them to fuck off with my attitude. I get it. I know they're worried about her, but I'm not that guy. Sure, they don't know that, but she's an adult. She can make her own choices. And, damn, they need to let her breathe a little.

We stop next to the hotel entrance, and Peyton turns to face me. "I'm sorry about that. They're... protective. It's a curse being the youngest."

"You have nothing to be sorry for," I say, tucking a flyaway hair behind her ear.

She nods and steps to the side, taking a seat on the bench. "Cameron Taylor is my brother-in-law. He's married to my eldest sister, Paisley."

"I caught that," I tease, bumping my arm into hers.

"And Holden, he and my sister Parker are dating. Well, more than dating, but they're not married."

"Caught that too."

"I'm sorry I didn't tell you." Her words are soft, and I can feel the regret rolling off her in waves. At least, I think it's regret.

"Hey." I turn and place my index finger under her chin and lift her eyes to mine. "You had no responsibility to tell me about your sisters' husband and boyfriend."

"But you love baseball, and you want to go pro." She pauses, and when I open my mouth to speak, she beats me to it. "Even though I'm sure you've figured it out, I guess I should also confess that my dad is Easton Monroe."

Fuck. I assumed when I learned her sister was married to Cameron Taylor. I know he was married to Easton Monroe's eldest daughter. They were all over the sports news stations when they first got together.

"I kind of put two and two together."

"Yeah," she says sadly.

"Hey." I wait for her to look at me. "What's going on in that pretty little head of yours?"

"I wanted you for me," she murmurs.

"What?" I hear her, but I'm not sure I understand what she's trying to say.

"It's stupid."

"Nothing you feel is stupid. Talk to me."

"I don't know you."

"Yet here you are sitting with me. What's going on, Peyton?"

"I wanted to be just Peyton. I didn't want you to see me as Easton Monroe's daughter or Cameron Taylor's sister-in-law. I just wanted to be Peyton."

"That's who you are to me. You're Peyton, the beautiful girl I met on the beach yesterday and has somehow managed to burrow her way inside my head. I can't stop thinking about you. That started before I knew who your family was."

"Yeah," she says, but I can tell by her tone that she doesn't believe a word that I'm saying.

"Pull out your phone," I tell her.

"What?"

"Come on, humor me. Pull out your phone." She does as I ask. "Now, open up our messages and read through them." She shakes her head as if she can't believe she's doing this, but she scrolls through our messages anyway. "Now, tell me that I'm not here for you."

"Oh my God," she breathes. I smile because she's finally getting it. "You knew. You knew who I was all along. How could I be so stupid? I let my guard down. Dammit." She stands and begins to walk away.

"Peyton!" I call out, running to catch up with her. "Hey, stop," I say, grabbing her wrist gently to get her to stop running away from me. She stops moving but doesn't turn to face me.

My heart thunders in my chest as I realize she could walk away and I'd never see her again. I don't want that to happen. That realization alone has my palms sweaty. I've never chased a girl, but something in my gut tells me that Peyton is worth it. She's unlike anyone I've ever met before. She's down to earth. She is who she is, and she's unapologetic about it. She's not one of those girls who refuse to eat in front of you. She's not constantly worrying about her appearance, messing with her hair and makeup; she's just Peyton. And although I've only known her for a very short amount of time, I know that I want to know more. I never want to know more.

Not knowing what else to do, I wrap my arms around her from behind, holding her close just like I did last night. "I didn't know," I whisper in her ear. "I didn't know who you were, and even if I did, it wouldn't have mattered to me."

"How can you say that?" She turns in my arms. Her brown eyes are full of sadness. "You don't know that."

"I do know that. I know you're the first girl I've ever met who I want to spend more time with. I've yet to ever meet someone who doesn't annoy the hell out of me with their fakeness until you. You've been nothing but real with me, and I want to learn more about you. I want to spend more time with you. You told me that you're here for five days. If my listening skills are correct, this is day three. That means I have today and two more to spend with you, and I'd like to do that if you'd let me?"

"Griffin—" she starts, but I stop her, pulling her into my arms for a hug. Her body fits perfectly next to mine. She just feels right.

"Let's move out of the front of the hotel," I whisper in her ear.

She nods and steps out of my hold. I don't let her get far. I slide my arm around her waist and walk her to the side of the hotel. Seeing a bench, I sit down and boldly pull her onto my lap.

"Is this okay?" I ask.

"Now you ask for permission?" she teases.

"I just wanted you close so that you can't escape, but I'd never force you to do anything you're not comfortable with."

"I believe you."

"Do you believe me that I didn't know who you were when we met?"

"You didn't even react in there, Griffin. There was no shock on your face."

"I was shocked, trust me, but I was trying to impress your family, Peyton. I didn't want them to think I was some fan using you. That's not who I am or what I'm doing."

"What would make you think that? You had to know who I was to come to the conclusion so quickly," she says, folding in on herself.

I hug her to me. "I read your body language. Your shoulders were tight, and you barely made eye contact with me. I could tell that you were uncomfortable with the situation, and the only thing I could think of was it was me being there. You didn't want me to come to your room, and it's my guess if I read the room correctly, Cameron and Holden weren't supposed to be there."

"Pretty much."

"Let me show you. Spend the day with me. Karina is probably waiting for us in the lobby."

"I live in Tennessee."

"I know, and that sucks, but that doesn't change the fact that I want to get to know you."

"This can't go anywhere."

Hearing her say those words brings out the competitive side of me. I want to prove her wrong. I'm starting to think that Oliver's right, and she did cast some kind of voodoo spell on me. "Please?"

She bites down on her bottom lip, and I can't help but wonder what those lips would feel like pressed to mine. "Okay. We can hang out."

"What about this?" I ask.

"What about what?"

"Can I hold you like this?" I ask, not even recognizing myself.

"Do you want to?"

"More than anything."

"I'm not sleeping with you. You can't pull out all of your charms to convince me otherwise."

"Who said anything about sleeping?" I tease.

"Sex, Griffin. There will be no sex."

"Get your mind out of the gutter," I fire back, pretending to be horrified.

"Stop." She laughs, pushing at my shoulder.

"I'm kidding. I just want to hold you. Like last night. I just want you close." For the first time in my life, I've found someone I don't want to let go of.

"This doesn't make any sense."

"Trust me, I know. I'm not this guy. I don't chase, and I don't beg for more time, but here I am."

"Why me?"

"Because I knew the minute I laid eyes on you that you were special. I felt it in my gut. It's a feeling I can't explain, and it's one I've never felt with anyone but you. I always trust my gut, Peyton. So even if this is out of character for me, I'm rolling with it."

Her only reply is to rest her head on my shoulder. I don't understand my reaction to her, but I meant what I said. My gut has never steered me wrong.

"Come on, let's go get Karina and head to my place. The guys are waiting on us," I say just as her phone rings. She stands and pulls it out of her purse and shows me the screen. She smiles when she places the phone to her ear.

"We'll be right there." She pauses. "Me and Griffin." Another pause. "I'll explain later." She ends the call and slides her phone back into her purse. I stand and offer her my hand, and she takes it.

I feel ten feet tall walking into that hotel to meet her best friend with her hand entwined with mine. I should be worried that this is happening too fast, but I can't seem to care when she's this close. Who am I kidding? I didn't care this morning when I couldn't stop thinking about her either.

I'm in trouble with this one.

"Look at you two," Karina says as we approach her.

Peyton tries to pull her hand away, but I hold strong. "Are we all set, ladies?" I ask them.

"Yep." Karina grins.

"Peyton? Do you have everything you need?" I look her in the eyes, making sure she knows she has my full attention. I don't know why, but it's important to me that she understands that it's her, not her family, and not her last name. Just her.

"Yes. My suit is on underneath this. Oh, I guess we should go get some towels from our rooms."

"No need. My mom has a million beach towels at our place. Sunscreen too."

"Well then, we're all set," Karina chimes in.

"I told Ollie to fire up the grill at noon. He's a master on the grill, at least he thinks he is. We pretend to go along with it." I laugh. "Anyway, he's going to throw on some burgers, and it should be ready or almost ready by the time we get there."

"Are your parents going to be there?" Peyton asks.

"They're out today. They're going out on the boat with some friends of theirs."

"Oh, you have a boat?" Karina asks.

"Yeah, my dad loves to fish."

"Do you? Love to fish, I mean?" Peyton asks.

"Yeah, it's something I grew up doing. Do you fish?"

"We live in Tennessee," Karina replies.

I toss my head back in laughter. "Just because you live in Tennessee doesn't mean you fish."

"Fair point," Karina agrees. "Yes, we both fish."

"Come on, we better head out before Ollie sends a search party."

"Aw, is he worried about you?" Karina asks.

"Nah, he's probably more worried about the two of you than me."

"Uh, not really convincing if you're wanting us to get into this Jeep with you, bud," Peyton says.

"That came out wrong. He's probably worried. I'm begging you all to come with me before I screw this up somehow."

"Why would you screw it up?" Peyton asks. She tilts her head to the side, exposing the long slender column of her neck, and I want to kiss her there.

"Because he knows me. I don't do this." I wave a hand between Peyton and me. "Sure, I've invited a group of girls over to hang with us, but it's them showing up. I don't even offer to pick them up."

"Yeah, but we're from out of town."

"So are some of the girls we go to school with."

"What your boy here is trying to say is that you're different."

"That." I point at Karina and nod.

"It's been a day." Peyton raises her eyebrows in challenge.

"A little over twenty-four hours if my calculations are correct," I counter.

"Come on, you two, let's get this show on the road. We're wasting this beautiful Florida sunshine." Karina opens the door and climbs into the back seat of my Jeep.

I stand by and wait for Peyton to settle in the passenger seat before closing her door and rushing around to the driver's side. "Ready?" I ask, glancing over at Peyton.

"Let's do it." Her tone is light, but I can still see the heaviness of the morning in her eyes. Today, I'm going to make it my mission to have that smile she's giving me turn into a genuine one, and I want it to reach her eyes. I want my Peyton from yesterday. I'll show her that it doesn't matter to me who her family is. They're not the people in my head, taking up every thought.

I only have her for three days. Two and a half technically, and I don't want to waste a single second of it.

CHAPTER 5
Peyton

"WHAT'S GOING ON WITH YOU?" Karina asks in a hushed voice.

We're on lounge chairs beside Griffin's pool. "Nothing." As soon as we arrived, Griffin led us to the backyard, and I hightailed it to the lounge chair, and this is where we've been ever since. I managed to pull off an entire twenty minutes or so of being lost in my head before Karina's question.

"Bullshit."

I should have known she wasn't going to let me get away with that reply. I don't even know why I tried. "Griffin wanted to come to the room to pick me up. He said he wanted it to be a proper date."

"And?"

"And I didn't want him to, but Parker overheard our conversation and said to let him come up... that she wanted to meet him."

"Did she hate him or something? Was he an ass to her?"

"No, nothing like that." I heave out a heavy sigh and go on to tell her about my morning.

"Damn, so he met Cameron and Holden?" she asks, even though I just told her that they did.

"Yep."

"And you're freaking out?"

"No. I mean, not really. I just wanted him for me, Karina. He didn't know who I was yesterday. I was just Peyton. Some random girl he met on spring break, and now I'm Peyton Monroe, daughter to Easton Monroe. Sister-in-law to Cameron Taylor. Soon-to-be sister-in-law to Holden Bailey. I just wanted to be me."

"Okay," Karina says, sitting up and moving to sit sideways on the lounge chair. "There is a lot I need to dissect with that little rant. However, let's start with Parker and Holden got engaged, and you didn't tell me?"

This makes me laugh. "No. They're not engaged, but I'm sure it's only a matter of time. Hell, even Holden said so himself earlier."

"Good for them." She nods, a happy smile pulling at her lips. "Now, back to you. You have always been Peyton Monroe. You were you yesterday, and you're you today." I start to argue, and she holds up her hand to stop me. "Now, before you go arguing the fact, I want you to think about something." She pauses and waits for me to nod my acceptance. "Yesterday, Griffin didn't know who you were, and he was still into you." I try to talk again, but she gives me a warning look, so I stay quiet. "Today, he's still into you."

"But," I interject, and this time she lets me, "what if he knew who I was yesterday?" I know I'm being irrational, but it's a real concern for me. Hell, it was a concern for my sisters too. Guys like them... like *us* for our connection to our dad, or Uncle Drew, and now even Cameron, and I guess Holden for me.

"Do you really think that, Peyton? Do you feel as though you've been played?"

I take a minute to think about her question. "No. I don't feel like I've been played, but what if I was?"

"What if you miss out on a great guy because you're paranoid?"

"It's not like anything could come of this," I remind her. "We live too far away. Long-distance relationships never work."

"Don't they? Look at your parents and your sisters. Sure, their relationships are not in the true sense of the word long-distance, but they fit the bill pretty closely. Your dad was gone all the time, and so are Cameron and Holden, but they all manage to make it work."

"That's different," I counter.

"How?"

"It just is."

"Hey, you ladies ready to eat?" Daniel appears next to us. He takes a seat on the lounge chair next to Karina and taps her leg with his. "It's ready," he tells us.

"It's about time; I'm wasting away over here." Karina stands in her tiny little red bikini. "Lead the way," she tells him.

His eyes rake over her body, and he grins. "Gladly." He stands as well and offers her his arm. Then he stops and turns to me. "You coming, Peyton?"

"Yeah. I just need to slip into my shorts." I stand to do just that, and his words stop me.

"Why would you cover that up?" He waves his hand that's not linked with Karina's up my body. "Wait, on second thought, Griff is helping Ollie with the grilling. I don't want my burgers burnt, so you might want to," he teases.

"I thought you said the food was done?" I ask.

"Oh, they were getting ready to pull the burgers off when I walked over here, but we shouldn't take any chances." He glances over the other side of the pool, where the outdoor kitchen is located. "Never mind, the food is off the grill. We're safe." He reaches for my hand and pulls me to him, linking his arm with mine. "This is the life," he boasts as we walk toward the table and the rest of the group.

"I picked this one up for you," Daniel says as we stop next to where Griffin is sitting at the table.

Griffin smiles, moves his chair back, and pulls me onto his lap. Don't get me wrong, I go willingly. "How are you doing?" he whispers low, just so I can hear him. His hand rests on my thigh, and since I'm sitting sideways, I don't have to turn much to see him.

"I'm fine." I smile, letting him know that I truly am okay. The heat from his hand on my thigh is so distracting that I can't really concentrate on replying much more than that. My body is very aware that I'm sitting on his lap in a tiny black bikini. Damn Daniel for not letting me put my shorts on. Griffin is wearing a pair of boardshorts, so there's not much between us, and I can feel him. My face heats, and not from embarrassment from my reaction to him meeting my family earlier today.

Sure, I wasn't ready for him to meet my family, but it's not a big deal. At least, that's what I keep telling myself. I'm here for two more days, and then I'll be heading home to Tennessee, back to college, and Griffin will just be a memory. He'll be the guy I met on spring break my freshman year of college. We'll follow each other on social media and like each other's posts. That's all this is. I might as well enjoy my time with him, make those memories that will stay with me forever.

"Are you hungry?" he asks, reaching over and grabbing me a paper plate.

"I'm starving, actually."

"Well, you're in for a treat."

"Oh, yeah?"

"I'm the grill master."

"I thought that was Oliver?" I tease.

"See." Oliver points a long finger at me. "Your girl knows what's up." He grins.

"He's not lying," Sam chimes in. "Griffin makes a mean steak on the grill."

"Hey." Oliver slaps his hand to his chest as if he's offended, but his smile and the laughter of his friends tells me otherwise.

"I'm more of a chicken kind of girl."

"What? You don't eat steak?" he asks.

"I do, but it's just not my favorite. It's tough, and I feel like I get a workout just trying to chew it."

"Then you need to have one of mine. They're so tender you can cut it with a fork."

"The only steak I've ever been able to cut with a fork is the baked steak my mom makes."

"Well, then you're going to have to either stick around for dinner or come back tomorrow so I can prove you wrong." He stares at me expectantly, waiting on my answer.

"All right, almighty grill master. You tell me when to be here, and we'll make it happen. I need to taste this steak I can cut with a fork."

"He's telling you the truth," Oliver speaks up. "His dad is a chef, so he's taught him a thing or two. Hell, he's taught me a thing or two," he admits.

"Good to know." I nod.

"It's all in the preparation and seasoning. We better count on dinner tomorrow night to give me time to prepare. I need to make sure I'm at my best," Griffin suggests.

"Tomorrow night it is," I agree.

I'm sitting sideways on his lap, and he leans in close. "How about just the two of us?" he asks.

"You wanting me all to yourself?" I tease.

"Yes." There is not one single ounce of hesitation in his reply.

"Date number two?"

He smiles. "Date number two."

"You want to go for a swim?" Griffin asks.

After we ate, he led me to the lounge chair I was sitting in earlier and pulled me next to him. We've been curled up watching our friends ever since.

"It is hot as hell out here." I'm burning up, but I didn't want to move from his arms either.

"I thought that was just because I was holding you."

"Smooth." I shake my head with a laugh.

"What?" He feigns innocence. "It's hot out here, and we were so close our body heat made it worse."

"Uh-huh, good attempt at a cover-up."

He gives me a cheeky grin. "All a part of my master plan. Get you all hot and sweaty," he says huskily. "Only to be able to cool you off."

Before I can stop him, he's lifting me into his arms, and then we're running. He doesn't pause before he launches his body and, by default, mine as I'm in his arms, over the side of the pool and into the deep end.

He releases me once we hit the water, and we both swim to the surface. "Not cool, Griffin Anthony. Not cool."

He swims closer. "Let me make it up to you." Gripping my waist, he pulls me close, and on instinct, I wrap my arms and legs around him while he keeps us afloat. He somehow manages to swim us to the shallow end of the pool, where he's able to stand. Then again, it might not be as shallow as I think. Griffin is well over six feet tall. His shallow and my five-foot-six shallow have different meanings.

"Not cool," I say again. My voice doesn't sound like my own. It's all breathy and seductive.

"I wish I could say I was sorry," he says, tightening his hold on my thighs. "But it got you here, and I can't be sorry about that."

Despite being in the pool, my body is still heated, and I know it's from his touch. He seems to be unaffected by my nearness, so I decide to try to level the playing field. Squeezing my legs tighter around his waist, I grind my core against him.

"Peyton," he groans.

"Yes?" I ask. My voice is the epitome of innocence. For the first time today, I feel as though I finally have the upper hand. That is until he adjusts his hips, and I can feel his hard length. We have two very thin layers of fabric separating us. It makes it easy to feel all of him.

"Oh," I say before I can stop myself.

"Peyton," he breathes, resting his forehead against mine. "You drive me crazy."

"You're hard to resist too," I say with a giggle.

His laugh is low and deep. "I can't help it. Not where you're concerned."

I pull back to look into his eyes. "So, you're telling me that this…" I wiggle my hips, and he groans. "Only happens with me?"

"No," he confesses. "But then again, you're the only girl I've had here in my pool and in my arms at the same time."

"Right." I laugh. "Come on now. Be real with me."

"We've had parties here, but I've never been with anyone during any of them. Not like this."

"I find that hard to believe."

"I don't know how to explain it without sounding like a conceited jerk."

"Try me."

He nods. "I've always been good at baseball. College scouts started coming to my games when I was a freshman in high school. Some girls catch on that something bigger than who's dating who that week is going on, and they want to latch on and ride the coattails to fame and fortune."

"I understand that more than you think."

"Yeah." He smooths my hair back out of my eyes. "I'm guessing that you do. Anyway, my high school coach, Coach Ratliff, was big on lecturing us. Don't be stupid. Wrap it before you tap it, watch your back, all those kinds of things. He was more than just a coach, he was a mentor of sorts. He preached to us about being careful."

"Sounds like a good guy."

"Yeah," he agrees. "So our sophomore year, a buddy of mine, Jack, he had a party at his house, drank too much, and passed out in his room. He woke up the next day with a naked girl lying next to him. She'd been chasing him for months, and he wouldn't give her the time of day. He was a beast on the football field, and the girl, Susie, just had that vibe about her."

"Something tells me I'm not going to like where this is going."

"She took advantage of him. We all saw him go to his room alone. She got pregnant."

"Wow," I breathe. Not that I should be surprised. I've heard similar stories my entire life growing up.

"Yeah. Things were bad for a while, and then she lost the baby."

"That's awful. I mean, I hate the way that she went about it, but losing the baby is bad too."

"It is. Jack kicked her ass to the curb. He was trying to make it work for the baby, but things didn't work out for them. That changed me. I didn't want to ever be in Jack's position. So, when we have parties, I'm selective on who gets invited. They're never huge or wild, and everyone leaves in a cab at the end of the night. I also lock my bedroom door even though the house is empty other than the guys and me, just as a precaution."

"And where are your parents?"

"Usually on weekend getaways. My dad is a chef and owns his own string of restaurants across the state. They travel a lot for that."

"I see, so you take full advantage of having the house all to yourself."

"Pretty much." He grins.

"Your story, it's your way of telling me you're one of the good ones?" I ask playfully.

"No. It's my way of telling you that you're different, Peyton."

"Your life is more like mine than I originally thought."

"How so?"

"Earlier when I told you I wanted you just for me." He nods. "I was afraid that your interest would change to my connection to the game you loved and my family, who could potentially open doors for you. You make me feel... seen. I wasn't ready to let that go just yet."

"You're seen, Peyton Monroe. Not because of your last name or your connection to baseball. You're beautiful and real. You aren't pretending to be someone you're not, and I don't know... There's just something in my gut that tells me you're the real deal."

"What you see is what you get."

"Exactly."

"I could be playing you."

"I considered that, but you're too nice. Too genuine during our conversations. You can't fake that."

"Or this?" I say, wiggling my hips again. His hard length is still standing proud between us, causing a delicious ache between my thighs.

"Definitely not fake," he says, leaning in and pressing a kiss to my cheek. "And all for you," he whispers in my ear.

"Hey! Stop hogging my bestie. Let's play chicken," Karina calls out.

"We need to stay in the water anyway," Griffin says sheepishly. "Although having you on my shoulders isn't going to do much to tamp down this desire I have for you."

"Looks like we're going to be waterlogged."

"Let's get this game over with, and then as bad as I hate to say this, I need to not touch you to get this under control."

"I'm sorry." I bite down on my bottom lip as he walks farther into the shallow end of the pool and sets me on my feet.

"I'm the one who should be apologizing."

"I like knowing that you want me," I confess. I don't know what's gotten into me. I'm never this bold or this open with guys.

"I want you, beautiful, but it's not just about my dick. You know that, right?"

"I don't know. It's hard to make that distinction," I tease.

He pulls me into his arms, hugging me. "It's you."

"I leave in two days."

"I know." He places a kiss on the top of my head, then dips down into the water, letting me climb onto his shoulders.

CHAPTER 6
Griffin

I T's JUST AFTER TEN BY the time I get home from dropping the girls off at their hotel. I wasn't ready to take them back, but Peyton was dead on her feet, and honestly, so am I. I slept like shit last night. I couldn't stop thinking about her. I'm sure tonight it's going to be difficult as well, even though I'm tanked.

"You're home early," Mom says as I walk into the living room.

"So are you," I tease her.

"Well, your dad and I were both ready to come home. The restaurant in Miami is doing well, so here we are," she explains.

"Now, your turn," Dad chimes in. "What are you doing home so soon? It looks like you had some people over."

"Yeah, Sam, Ollie, and Daniel were here. And, uh, Peyton and Karina." I don't keep things from my parents. They're my sounding board in this crazy roller coaster called life.

"Do we know Peyton and Karina?" Mom asks.

"Nope." I know she's dying to ask me more, but she's trying to be chill and not grill me for details. I don't know why. We all three know she's going to cave and ask.

"It's killing you, isn't it?" Dad asks her.

"Yes!" She laughs. "Okay, where did you meet them? Are you interested in either of them? Tell me all the things." She moves to sit up straighter on the couch, placing her e-reader on the end table.

"We met them on the beach yesterday. They're here on spring break, and yeah, I think I might be."

"Whoa. I wasn't expecting that," Dad says.

"I wasn't expecting her." The confession rolls off my lips easily.

"All the things, Griffin," Mom reminds me.

"We hung out yesterday. She's easy to talk to and to be around." She also takes my breath away every time I look at her, but I keep that information to myself.

"Go on." Mom's smile is bright.

"I like her." I shrug, knowing it's going to drive her crazy.

"Ugh, why must you torture me?" she moans.

"Come on, Anna, give the kid some time to tell us about her."

"Gary Anthony, you leave me be," she scolds playfully.

Did I mention that my parents are couple's goals? They met in college and have been together ever since. Well mom was in college and dad was in culinary school. They still make each other laugh, and anyone who sees them together can practically feel the love radiating between the two of them. It's most definitely a sight to see.

"She's... I don't really know. I can't put it into words," I tell them.

"Can we meet her?" Mom asks.

"She lives in Tennessee. She's here for two more days, and then she's going back to school. She plays softball, and the season starts when she gets back."

"Oh, she plays softball. That's good. She understands the pressure and the commitment that you have to baseball," Mom comments.

"That's just it. She's tightly connected to the baseball world." That's the understatement of the century, but I don't really know how else to describe it. She's so tightly connected; it's who she is.

"Well, she plays, that's not exactly tightly connected," Dad chimes in.

"No, you don't get it. Her dad played for the majors. Her brother-in-law plays for the majors, and her soon-to-be brother-in-law also plays for the majors. They play for the same team that her dad played for."

"Damn," Dad mutters.

"I'd say that passes for being tightly connected," Mom agrees.

"Who's her dad?" mine asks.

"I don't want to say. I met her brother-in-law and soon-to-be this morning when I picked her up, but she didn't mean for me to. It was kind of an 'in the right place at the right time' kind of situation."

"Why did she not want you to meet them?" Mom sounds hurt.

"She said she wanted me to be hers." My heart hammers in my chest when I think about those words. What she doesn't realize is that I want to be hers too. I don't give a damn who her family is. I just want her.

"Aw," Mom coos.

"Meaning?" Dad asks.

I go on to tell them a little about our conversation. "I really like her."

"Then what's stopping you?" Dad asks.

"She lives so far away." Even with the almost thirteen-hour drive, and that's with no stops, I've been running plans through my head and dates of when I might be able to go visit her.

"Tennessee isn't that far. What part of Tennessee?" he asks.

"Nashville. It's a twelve-and-a-half-hour drive." I've put it into the GPS on my phone more times than I care to admit. I guess I was hoping that maybe I entered it wrong all the times before, and she would suddenly live closer. Wishful thinking on my part.

Dad nods. "Okay. So that's a long drive, but not impossible."

My parents are always my biggest supporters, no matter the challenge or situation.

"I have school and baseball. I don't know when I'd ever be able to get to see her. She has softball and school. It's as if we're doomed from the start."

"I've never heard you talk about a girl like you do her. I've never actually heard you admit that you like someone." Mom smiles. "That tells me she's special. Don't let a little distance stop you from pursuing something with her."

"It's impossible." I've done nothing but mull this over since the minute I laid eyes on her. I knew she was different.

"Nothing is impossible if you put the hard work and effort into it," Dad tells me. "Think of this just like you do baseball. Relationships take work. They're hard and messy, and they can also be the best thing in your life," he says, his eyes softening when he looks over at my mom.

"Right. You two make it look easy," I tell them.

"Maybe." Dad shrugs. "But it's work. You have to communicate, and when you're with someone and know them better than they know themselves, that means that you know how to get under their skin better than anyone. You know the words to cut deep."

"You two don't do that."

"We do," Mom says. "We have. We try not to, but it's human nature to take bad moods or sadness out on those we're closest to. We know that they'll be there no matter what."

"I don't even know if she's willing to start something."

"But haven't you already?" Mom asks.

"Not really. We're just hanging out."

"When do you see her again?" Dad asks.

"Tomorrow night. I'm supposed to be making her a steak. She says it's too much work to chew, and the guys told her that mine aren't like that."

"You're welcome," Dad boasts, making us laugh.

"Can we meet her? You did meet her family after all." Mom gives me a pleading look. I know she's been waiting for a time when I would bring someone home. Neither one of us ever thought it would be this complicated when it finally happened.

"I don't know. I don't want you scaring her away."

"I'll do no such thing." Mom raises her hands as if she's being sworn in under oath.

"I'll ask her. Maybe you all can be here for dinner with us tomorrow night?"

"We'd love that. You and I can take care of making dinner for our girls," Dad says, already making plans.

"She's not my girl." And for the first time in my life, I want to call someone my girl. I feel like I'm living in an alternate universe. This isn't me. I don't chase after girls, and I don't lose sleep over them either.

"Well, we'll help with that too." He laughs.

"No. No. No." I shake my head. "I don't need help. Let me see how she feels about it."

"Let us know," Dad says.

With that, I stand and kiss Mom on the cheek, giving her a hug. I'm feeling a little sentimental after our talk, so instead of a fist bump, Dad gets a hug, too, before I head up to my room.

I don't bother turning on the light. Instead, making my way to my bed in the dark, I plop down and pull out my phone. I debate on texting her or calling her, and calling wins. I just left her, and I already wanted to hear her voice.

Maybe I was abducted by aliens?

Shaking out of the thought, I pull up her name and tap the call button.

"Do you miss me already?" she greets me.

"Yes." I don't think about my answer or how desperate it might make me sound until the words are out of my mouth. Oh, well, honesty is the best policy.

"It hasn't even been an hour."

"Too long, Peyton." I'm smiling, knowing I've caught her off guard. "What are you doing?"

"I was sitting out in the living area talking to Holden, Cameron, and Parker, but when you called, I came to my room."

"Do you want me to let you go?"

"Do you want to let me go?"

"Never."

"I'm good," she says softly.

"So I was talking to my parents, and they'd like to meet you."

"Really?" she asks, surprise evident in her tone.

"Yeah. I thought maybe they could join us for dinner tomorrow night."

"I'm leaving, Griffin."

"I know." We're both quiet, and I finally speak again. "Did you know that it's a twelve-and-a-half-hour drive from here to Nashville?"

"How do you know that?"

"I told you I had a hard time sleeping last night. I looked it up."

"That's a long drive."

"But a short flight," I counter.

"What are you trying to say, Griffin?"

"I don't really know, to be honest. I know that I like you more than any girl I've ever met, and the thought of you leaving in two days and never seeing you again doesn't sit well with me."

"Long-distance relationships rarely work."

"You have to want it."

"Do you? Want one, I mean?"

"Yeah, Peyton. I think I do."

"This is crazy. We just met."

"I know. And I'm not proposing marriage. But I think we should at least consider it."

"Consider what exactly?"

"Seeing each other again."

"We have school and ball. I'm not sure when that would be."

"I know." I sit up, resting my elbows on my knees, running my hands through my hair. "I'm aware that it sounds like I've lost my mind. I am. I just... my gut tells me that if I let you leave without a promise of at least keeping in touch and seeing what might happen with us, I'd regret it." She's quiet, but I can hear her breathing. I don't push her to answer me. I know that this is intense and crazy as hell. We barely know each other, but my gut never steers me wrong.

"Let's just take the next two days and see what happens. I don't want expectations or plans for what could possibly happen in the future hanging over our heads. I just want to spend some time with this great guy I met and make some memories with him."

"Done."

She laughs. "That was easy."

"I didn't even mean to have this conversation with you tonight. It just kind of happened."

"You can't take it back, Anthony," she teases.

"I don't want to take it back, Monroe. In case you missed it, I'm trying to keep you tethered to me."

"I caught that," she replies.

"About tomorrow?"

"If you want me to meet them, I will. It's fair after the interrogation my family gave you."

"I want you to meet them. Dinner, and then we can leave, or go down to the basement and watch a movie, or whatever you want. I can take you back to the hotel, but I'd really like for you to meet them."

"Then I'll meet them."

"Thank you." I don't know why it feels as though a weight has been lifted from my shoulders, but it does. I guess I wanted her to meet them more than I thought I did.

"So, you ready for the season?" she asks.

"I stay ready," I quip, and she laughs. I love the sound. "What about you?"

"Definitely. I'm a little nervous, this being my first year playing in college. Both of my sisters did it, so I can too."

"Of course you can."

"I appreciate your faith in me."

"You're welcome. You're going to have to send me your schedule, and I'll see if I can make it to a game."

"I thought we weren't talking about the future?" she jokes.

"I can't seem to stop myself where you're concerned."

"What are you doing tomorrow during the day?"

"I have steaks to marinate."

"Yeah, right. Your parents are going to be there. You're going to get your dad to cook them."

"Nope. I have already told him what I promised you. I don't break my promises, Peyton."

"Well, I'm ready to cut this steak with a fork."

"You're going to love it."

"We'll see."

"What are your plans for tomorrow?"

"I'm not sure yet. I know that Cameron and Holden have the day off from training. Well, kind of. They have to go in early in the morning, and then they said they'll be done by noon or so. I think Karina is going to visit family. She has an aunt and uncle who live here."

"You're not going?"

"She invited me. I don't want to risk not being back in time for our dinner."

"Date number two."

"For date number two," she amends.

"This is where I should be the nice guy and tell you we can move the date to the next day, but you're leaving the day after that, and I want to be selfish. I want all the Peyton time you're willing to give me before you head home."

"Yeah," she agrees. "I'm growing kind of partial to Griffin time as well."

"My work here is done."

Her laughter flows through the line, and I'm surprised that I can see her eyes sparking in my mind and the long slender column of her neck as it tilts back. Two days with her, and I have her features memorized. I'm in trouble. Big trouble. I'm falling for this girl, and I should stop it. I should walk away, but instead, I'm running toward her, holding on to her with all that I have.

She yawns, and I know I need to let her go. "I guess I need to hit the hay. I have a big date tomorrow."

"Sorry. I know I keep yawning. I didn't sleep well last night."

"Me either, and I doubt I will tonight either."

"I hope that you do."

"Sweet dreams, Peyton."

"Good night," she says, and the line goes dead.

So. Much. Trouble.

CHAPTER 7
Peyton

For the second night in a row, I barely slept. I have too much nervous energy and excitement to sleep. That's why it's eleven, and I'm just now dragging my tired ass out of bed. I heard Parker up earlier, but I just rolled over and went back to sleep.

I take my time in the shower. I don't know what's going to happen tonight, but I want to be prepared for anything where Griffin and our date are concerned. His parents are going to be there, so I doubt I needed to even worry about it, but I'm not going to get caught with my panties down when it comes to being groomed. No pun intended.

I decide to ask Parker to braid my hair. She used to do it for me all the time growing up. My plan is to take it down before going to Griffin's, and it will have that nice beachy wave look. Grabbing a comb and a hair tie, I set off to find my sister.

"Morning, sleepyhead," she greets me.

"Sorry. I didn't sleep well last night."

"What's going on?" she asks.

"Nothing." I wave off her concern. "Do you mind French braiding my hair?"

"Sure." She sits up, and I take a seat between her legs on the floor. "It's been ages since I've done this. I hope I remember how."

"You don't braid Autumn's hair?"

"I have, but it's been a long time."

"Thanks for letting me tag along with you and for going to bat with Mom and Dad."

"Of course. Are you having a good time? I'm trying not to be a helicopter sister." She laughs, and it reminds me so much of our mom.

"I am. It's been nice to get away."

"And Griffin?"

"He's good," I admit.

"You really like this guy."

"Yeah. Just my luck, right? I meet someone I might actually be interested in, and he lives almost thirteen hours away."

"You've checked?"

"No. He did."

"Interesting."

"What? What does that mean?"

"Just that he sounds like he's into you as well."

"Yeah, he says he wants to keep in touch."

"Just keep in touch? No long distance?"

"I told him I didn't want to talk about it for the next two days. That we should just focus on the here and now."

"Look, Peyton. I know that I should be telling you that you're young and you have plenty of time to find the one, but I'm not going to do that. You're only three years younger than me. I can tell you that if I had met Holden my freshman year, I would have had the same response to him then as I do now. When you know, you know."

"I don't know anything."

"Sure you do. You know, you just aren't willing to admit it to yourself."

"Come on, Parker. You do realize how insane this sounds, right?" My defense is weak even to my own ears.

"Maybe it seems that way to people who aren't living it. Trust me. There is no timeline for these kinds of things. Love at first sight is a real thing."

"Hold up, Parker. No one said anything about love."

"Fine. Lust, strong like, all of it, exists. It's what you do with those feelings that matter. Don't worry about anyone but you."

"Dad will flip his shit."

She laughs. "You're right. He will. But he'll also adjust. He did it with Paisley, and he did it with me. He'll do it with you."

"You were both older than me."

"I'm three years older, and if you remember, Paisley was right out of college too when she met Cam."

Before I get a chance at a rebuttal, the room to our suite opens, and Holden's voice fills the small space.

"Honey, I'm home," he calls out.

I hear male laughter, and I don't have to see Cameron to know that he's tagged along. However, I'm surprised when Uncle Drew steps into our suite as well.

"Did Dad send you?" I ask Drew.

He chuckles. "No. Well, he mentioned it, but Cam and Holden lured me here on the promise of dinner with two of my favorite girls."

I eye him suspiciously. "I'm watching you," I say, pointing my finger at him.

"You're all set," Parker says, tapping me on the shoulder.

I move to stand and hug Uncle Drew. He's not really our uncle, but he and my dad have been best friends way before any of us were thought of, so by default, he's Uncle Drew. "Are you having a good time?" he asks.

"She's having a blast," Cameron speaks for me.

Here we go.

"Oh, yeah? That's good, right?" Drew asks. He's clearly confused, which means Cameron and Holden haven't told him about Griffin.

"She met someone," Holden adds helpfully. "Ouch," he says when Parker smacks at his chest. He pulls her to him and kisses her. We all know my sister didn't hurt a hair on his head.

Drew studies me. "You're being safe, right, Peyton?"

My face heats. "Stop! We are not having this conversation," I tell him.

"That's not what I meant, but yeah, that too. I just mean you're a young girl on spring break. You don't know this guy."

"We met him," Cameron speaks up. "Seems like a good kid."

"Agreed." Holden nods.

"See. I'm fine."

"In fact, why don't you call him and have him join us for lunch?" Cameron suggests.

"Nope. He's making me dinner tonight. His dad is a chef, so they're kind of both making dinner for his mom and me," I say, clamping my mouth shut. I've already said too much. This nosy bunch is going to ask questions.

"You should call him," Parker urges. "You never know until you ask."

I bite down on my bottom lip. I want to see him. I want to spend as much time with him as I can over the next two days.

But do I really want him here with my family? He proved that he could be around them and not act a fool yesterday. Besides, my family is my rock. They're my team, so to speak. They can spend some time with him and let me know what they think. His family will get that with me tonight, so I should at least offer it to him.

"Fine. But I'm warning you three." I point at all three men. "Do not embarrass me."

"Hey, what about your sister?" Holden asks, laughing. "She's the one you have to worry about."

"No, I don't have to worry about Parker. She's been in my shoes with you." I point at Holden. "Please, can you not grill him? Please?"

"We'll be on our best behavior," Drew assures me.

Somehow, I feel like he's pulling my chain, but I tug my phone out of my pocket anyway. I scroll to Griffin's contact and hit call as I walk into my bedroom and close the door.

"Morning, beautiful. I wanted to text that, but I didn't want to wake you, and then Dad and I got busy preparing for tonight. How did you sleep?" he rambles.

"Morning, or afternoon, rather," I answer. "I was up a good part of the night."

"Me too," he confesses.

"So you're prepping, huh?" I can't take him away from that. Our dinner tonight was planned first.

"We were. It's all done until it's time to start cooking later. What are you getting into?"

"Well, Holden and Cameron are here, and my uncle Drew. We're going to a late lunch."

"Sounds like fun."

"They're a riot. That's for sure."

"Sounds like you all are close."

"We are, which is kind of why I'm calling. It was their idea, but I want you to come. Anyway, the guys suggested I see if you wanted to come to lunch with us today?"

"Do you want me there, Peyton?"

"I just said that I did."

"If you feel pressured to ask me, I won't do it."

"I want you to come with us, but you have to promise me something."

"Anything."

"They're protective. I don't want them to scare you off."

"Not a chance."

"Then I'd love for you to come to lunch with my family." I find the words to be true as I say them. Sure, I'd like to keep him just for me, but the cat is already out of the bag, so to speak, so there's no use in hiding that I'm into him, even if this ends when I go back home.

"Tell me when and where I need to be, and I'll make it happen."

"I'm not sure. How about you just head this way?"

"I'm heading out the door now. I'll just come up to your room."

"Okay. That works. Are you sure you want to do this?"

"Let me see. Am I sure that I want to spend the rest of the day with this beautiful girl I recently met and can't stop thinking about? Hell yes," he says, answering his own question, making me smile.

"I'll see you soon, Griffin."

"Ten minutes tops." The line goes dead, and I fall back onto my bed.

I can't believe I just did that. Yesterday, I was freaking out about him meeting Cameron and Holden, and now I'm inviting him to do so, and Uncle Drew is here. I'm not naïve enough to think Drew's not going to call my dad and fill him in. Those two are thick as thieves. I just set myself up for an interrogation when I get home. Possibly sooner. I did it willingly, all just to spend more time with him.

Knowing that if I don't get out there and fill them in, the four of them will come to me, I climb to my feet, slide my phone back in my pocket, and head back to the living area.

"Well?" Parker asks.

"He's on his way."

"All right." Holden rubs his hands together.

"I swear on everything holy, if you embarrass him or me, I'm never babysitting for you," I warn him.

"You might want to hold back," Cameron tells him. "She's helped us out more times than I can count with Jett."

"You wouldn't do that. You'd be depriving yourself of niece and nephew time," Holden counters.

"That's how important this is to me," I admit.

"I'll have his ass running sprints if he does," Drew speaks up.

"Damn," Holden mutters. "Fine. I'll be good. As long as he's good to you, that is."

"I can live with that." Griffin is good to me. Opening doors and leading me into rooms good to me. I can't imagine my family will have an issue with any of that.

"So, where are we headed?" Drew asks.

"A restaurant not far from here. Some of the guys were talking about it. They went last week and said the food was out of this world," Cameron tells him as there's a knock on the door.

The sound seems to drown out all other noise in the room. Maybe that's because it does. Everyone goes quiet and looks at me expectantly. "I'll get it," I mutter, making my way to the door. I pull it open to see Griffin's smiling face. He looks good. He's wearing khaki shorts, a polo, and boat shoes. His shaggy brown hair is slicked back, making his brown eyes sparkle.

"Hey, beautiful," he whispers, but from the "Aw" I hear come from my sister behind me, I know they heard him.

"Come on in," I say, stepping back. "I hope you're ready for this."

"You're here. Of course I am." He winks, and my heart flutters in my chest.

Closing the door, I move to stand next to him. "Guys, this is Griffin. Griffin, you met all but Uncle Drew yesterday, but I'll go through introductions again just in case."

"I'm good, Peyton." He offers his hand to my sister again. "Nice to see you again, Parker. Thank you for inviting me."

"Nice to see you too. You remember Holden and Cameron?" she asks.

"I do. Nice to see you again." He offers both of them his hand to shake as well. "You must be Drew. I'm Griffin. Nice to meet you."

"You as well."

"So, are we ready to go?" I ask the group.

"Hold up, ladies, you need to change. This place says it has a dress code," Cameron says, reading from his phone. He looks up at Griffin. "Have you ever been to Anthony's? Do they really need to change?" he asks.

Griffin smiles. "That's actually my dad's restaurant. Let me call them and see if the back room is available. If so, we can go as we are." Griffin pulls his phone out of his pocket and makes the call. "Hey, Macey, it's Griffin. Hey, can you tell me if the back room is open today?" He pauses. "Perfect. Can you put me down for six for the next three hours, please?" Another pause. "Great, thanks. Hey, is my dad there today?" He laughs. "Yeah, let him know I'll be there with Peyton and some of her family. Thanks, Macey." He slides his phone back into his pocket before addressing Cameron. "The back room is ours. No dress code is required. We can go in through the back."

"Are you sure?"

"Positive."

"You're not going to get into trouble with your dad for this, are you?" I ask him.

"No. Not at all. He's not working in the kitchen today, but he is there. I know you were going to meet him tonight, but don't be surprised if he stops in to say hello."

"No pressure," I grumble, and he laughs as he slides his arm around my shoulder and presses his lips to my temple. "They're going to love you," he assures me.

"Right. So, shall we go?" Parker asks. My sister knows this is uncomfortable for me. Having all of them here with Griffin. A guy I just met but feel as though I've known a lifetime.

"Let's do this."

Together we make our way to the elevator. Griffin, as suspected, places his hand on the small of my back and leads me out of our room and down the hall to wait for the elevator. Cameron, Drew, and Holden ask him about baseball, and he talks to them as if they were just strangers off the street. He doesn't seem to be starstruck by their positions with the Blaze. I move to stand a little closer to him, and he slides his arm around my waist. I knew he was different. And I know what the sport means to him, so this has to be a big deal, but he's taking it in stride. He's not fanning all over them. They're just my family, who happen to be the general manager and two starting players for a Major League baseball team.

"How are we driving over?" Holden asks.

"I have my rental."

"The three of us have one too," Parker points out as we step onto the elevator.

"I have my Jeep too," Griffin adds.

"We don't all need to drive," Parker comments.

"Okay, well, Griffin and I are going to drive separately. Whoever else can follow us since we're taking the back entrance.

Sound good?" I ask as we step off the elevator. We make our way outside as the conversation of who is driving continues.

"Where are you parked?" Drew asks Griffin.

"There." Griffin points at his Jeep parked in front of the hotel.

"I'm right beside you. Let's just take mine," Drew says and starts walking toward his car while Griffin and I head to his Jeep. "We're right behind you," Drew calls out to us.

Griffin walks me to the passenger side of his Jeep and opens the door for me. "It's really good to see you, Peyton," he says before closing the door and making his way to his side.

"I'm sorry in advance for anything the four of them say or do while we are having lunch."

"It's fine, Peyton. I promise I can handle it."

"Do you have a lot of experience with this kind of thing? Meeting the family?"

"No. I already told you that I don't."

"Then how could you possibly know that you can handle it?"

"Because you're going to be there with me. I'm pretty damn sure I could endure a whole hell of a lot just to get to sit next to you."

"You can't say things like that," I blurt as I place my hand over my quivery belly.

"What? Why not? It's the truth."

"Because it causes my belly to be queasy."

"Good queasy or bad queasy?" he asks.

"Good. Like a swarm of butterflies." I feel stupid for saying any of that out loud, but the smile he gives me tells me he's glad I did.

"Noted." He winks as he pulls out onto the road.

CHAPTER 8
Griffin

I HAD NO IDEA WHAT I was getting myself into when Peyton called earlier. What I did know was that she was asking to spend time with me, and considering tomorrow is her last day here, I was all in.

It turns out her family is pretty amazing. I've been sitting here in the back room of my father's restaurant talking to her uncle and brothers-in-law like we've known each other for years. Parker and Peyton keep up with the conversation like pros, and I like this girl even more, knowing how much she not only knows about the game that I love but how much she seems to love it too.

Our plates are empty, and our bellies are full. I'm holding Peyton's hand under the table, and although it makes me feel as if I'm back in middle school, I'm not willing to let go either. I'm already counting down how many hours I have left with her, and I do not like the number.

"Well, we should get going," Parker says, standing. "I know that the two of you have plans later."

"Not until dinner," I speak up. I look over at Peyton. "She doesn't think I can make a steak tender enough to cut with a fork," I tell her family.

"I'm just saying I've never had that before."

"Well, if the meal today was any indication, my guess is he's going to prove you wrong." Drew smiles at us.

"Are you all done for the day?" Peyton asks them.

"Yes, and I'm headed to the hotel to video call my family." Cameron reaches for his wallet as the server comes in. He tries to hand him his card, telling him to put it all on his.

"I'm sorry, sir. Mr. Anthony has insisted that today's meal be on the house," Todd, a longtime employee of Anthony's, tells him.

"Did you do this?" Cameron asks me.

"No. But I'm not surprised by it either. That's just my dad." I shrug. "In fact, I'm shocked he didn't stop in and say hi, but I'm sure he was respecting your family time. He knows we get Peyton to ourselves tonight."

"Please thank him for us." Parker smiles at me.

I nod. "I'll be sure to tell him."

Cameron reaches into his wallet and pulls out a wad of cash, then hands it to Todd. "This is for you. Thank you for a great meal and service," he tells him.

We stand, and I make it a point to go to Parker first. Instead of shaking her hand, I pull her into a hug. "It was nice to meet you," I tell her.

"Hey, now, hands off my girl," Holden says. He's joking, but I also think he's half serious.

I laugh it off and offer him my hand and do the same with Cameron and Drew. I step back and stand next to Peyton. I want to entwine my fingers with hers, but I've already pushed the boundaries, and I don't want her family to think I'm going to maul her to death. That's not what this is. Not to mention that it's only been days, and I shouldn't feel this need to touch her and be near her. Not this soon.

"Are you coming back to the hotel?" Parker asks her sister.

Peyton looks up at me for direction. "My mom's at the house. We can head over there if you want?"

"Yeah, that sounds good," she agrees, turning to look at her sister. "We're going to head on over to Griffin's."

"I have the address," Parker assures her.

"Wait." This comes from Drew. "You have his address?" he asks, pointing at me.

"Of course I do. She went over there yesterday, and no way was I letting her go to some strange guy's house and me not know how to find her."

"Your dad would be so proud," Drew boasts.

Parker winks at Peyton. "Us Monroe girls have to stick together."

"Trust me," Holden says, "they do stick together."

"Get used to it," Cameron says as if it's a forgone conclusion that Peyton is mine.

I like it.

"It's good to know she's got support."

"You have no idea," Peyton mutters, and everyone laughs.

"Be safe and have fun," Parker says, hugging her sister.

"Always." She looks up at me. "Ready?"

"If you are." She nods, and this time, I do reach out to touch her. I place my hand on the small of her back and lead her out of the room. I know that her family is behind us, but I can't seem to find it in me to care. I really like this girl, and I can't help myself where she's concerned.

"Is your mom really home?" Peyton asks once we're in my Jeep and headed toward my place.

"She is. At least she's supposed to be." I reach over and place my hand on her thigh. "Hey, we don't have to go yet if you don't want to," I tell her.

"No. It's fine. I was just curious."

"I won't lie to you. Ever," I assure her.

"I don't trust easily. I've seen my sisters go through guys who used them, and even though they've both found their perfect match, I'm still a little skeptical, you know?"

"I get it. Your family is in the spotlight, and I can't even imagine the assholes who have tried to use you to get to them."

"I'm glad you're not one of them," she says, surprising me.

"I'm glad you can see that I'm not."

"I was worried when you first met Cam and Holden, but you proved me wrong. Or I guess you could be a damn good actor."

"I'm real with you. Always. You get me straight to my core."

"You're going to make some girl very happy someday," she muses.

"Not you?"

"We live so far away from one another, Griffin. I don't see how this could work."

"Are we allowed to talk about it today?" I tease her.

"You know what? Maybe we should leave this topic of discussion off the table today as well."

"Nah, we're talking about it," I insist, pulling into my driveway. I climb out of my Jeep and meet her at her door, holding out my hand to help her.

"I can get in and out of vehicles on my own, you know?" She chuckles.

"I'm sure you can, but you won't if I'm around."

"Aw, I did do something right." I hear my mom say.

I turn to look over my shoulder and find her standing on the front porch. "Hey, Mom. What are you doing?"

"I heard you pull up."

"Uh-huh. More like you talked to Dad or someone from the restaurant, and they saw us leave together."

"Griffin." She laughs. "The poor girl is going to think I'm a stalker or something." Mom steps off the porch and meets us halfway. "You must be Peyton. I'm Anna. It's so nice to meet you," she says, pulling Peyton into a hug.

"You too," Peyton says.

When Mom pulls back, they're both smiling. "I'm going to run to grab a few things from the store. Do you need anything?" she asks.

"No. Do you need help?"

She waves me off. "No, I won't be gone long," she says, turning to walk back into the house, with us following along behind her. She grabs her purse from the kitchen counter and waves as she disappears into the garage.

"She's nice," Peyton says.

"She is. Dad's cool too. I got lucky in the parent department."

"I did too," she agrees. "Sure, my dad can be overprotective, but it's not just with my sisters and me. It's with my mom too. He even has these silly names for us."

"This I've got to hear," I say, taking her hand in mine and leading her down to the basement. "You want something to drink?" I offer, remembering my manners.

"No thanks."

I lead her to the huge sectional couch we have and sit, pulling her into my lap. "Now, tell me more about these ridiculous names."

"It's crazy. He's crazy when it comes to the four of us, but it's crazy love if that makes any sense."

"Yeah, I think I get it. My dad is that way with my mom."

"Not you?"

"Well, to an extent. I'd imagine if I had a sister, he'd be the same with her."

She mumbles something about double standards, making me laugh. "It's not funny." She crosses her arms over her chest.

"I'm sorry," I tell her. "You're just cute as hell when you're frustrated. Now, names. Start talking, woman," I say, patting her thigh with my hand.

"He calls my mom queen."

I nod. "That's not bad at all. And it makes sense. She's his queen." I shrug.

"Oh, it gets worse. I started out with the not-so-crazy one."

"Lay it on me, Monroe," I say.

"He calls my older sister Paisley, princess. Parker is duchess, and he calls me lady."

"Fucking genius."

"What?"

"It's perfect. You don't like it?"

"Doesn't it seem, I don't know? Pretentious?"

"No. You four are the most important people in his life. I get it."

"You get my dad's brand of crazy. He'd love you."

"You think I'll ever get the chance to meet him?" I ask, and she stiffens. "I don't want to meet Easton Monroe, the baseball player. I want to meet the man who dubbed you lady. I want to meet him as your father."

"They're one and the same."

"Then why did you stiffen up on me?" We both know why she did it.

"Hard habit to break, I guess."

"You don't trust me yet."

"I do," she counters.

"Not enough, and that's okay. I'll prove it to you."

"You've got your work cut out for you. I leave the day after tomorrow."

"Ah, yes, thanks for bringing that up. I think we should keep in touch."

"Okay."

She agreed to that way too easily, which means she does not understand what I'm saying. "Peyton." I wait for her eyes to lock with mine. "I want us to do more than just keep in touch. I think we should try it."

"Try what exactly?" she asks, moving off my lap. I don't want to let her go, but maybe that's what she needs for this conversation. She's now sitting next to me, on her knees, staring at me with wide expressive eyes. She wants this too. I can see it. But she's also scared, and I understand that as well.

"I think we should try long distance." I feel like a fifty-pound weight has been lifted off my shoulders now that the words are out there.

"That's crazy," she says, but it's not convincing.

"Is it? Sure, we just met, but you're the first girl I've ever met who sees me for me, and I'm not ready to let that go just yet."

"Yeah," she agrees, her voice soft.

"So, what do you think?"

"How is this going to work? Griffin, we'd never get to see each other."

I run my fingers through my hair. "I stayed up all night last night thinking about it. We won't get a lot of time with each other during these next four years, but after that, we'll have all the time in the world. Well, unless I get picked up, then I'll be traveling a lot, but for home games and all that, I'll be home."

"When you get picked up," she says, giving me a look that dares me to challenge her. "It could be anywhere. That would still be long-distance."

"You could come with me."

"This is absolutely insane, Griffin. We barely know each other."

"Then let's start with that. We agree not to see other people right now and take the time to get to know one another. We can video call, and talk on the phone, and text, and email. Hell, we can go the snail-mail route if you want. We'll take the time to get to know each other, and then we can go from there."

She shakes her head. "That's a pretty big commitment for two people who just met."

"I agree." I take her hand in mine. "It's also going to be hard as hell to watch you drive away from me the day after tomorrow."

"I have to go back."

"I know you do. I know that our lives are in two different locations, but I think our minds and maybe even our hearts are on the same path."

"You have girls throwing themselves at you all the time." She bites down on her bottom lip.

"I do," I agree. "And the first one not to is the one that I want to keep." Her eyes soften, and I can tell I've got her. She's going to give us a chance. I'm going to have to fight like hell to be the man she deserves with so many miles between us, but I'm up for the challenge, especially when Peyton Monroe is my reward.

"Can I think about it?" she asks, and my heart sinks. She must notice because she's quick to defend her question. "I just need to wrap my head around this. I need to let it sink in that you want me. Not just for while I'm here but for… longer."

"I'll make you a deal. You don't have to decide right away if you'll take a nap with me."

"Seriously?" she asks.

"I've barely slept since the day I met you, and I'm exhausted. I think knowing that you're here with me, I'll be able to sleep."

"That's not what I expected. I slept in today, but I could still use a nap."

I stand from the couch, and she does the same, following my lead. I adjust the pillows on the other side of the sectional and lay down, patting the space in front of me.

"Here?"

"Right here." I pat the space a second time. She moves to settle in next to me, and I wrap my arms around her. Placing a kiss on her temple, I close my eyes and soak up the feeling of having her in my arms like this. This moment feels right. *She* feels right. It kills me that I have one more day with her, and then I don't know when I'll get to see her again, but my gut tells me I need to hold this girl with both hands. I need to fight to convince her that taking the time for us to get to know each other better, even over the distance, is the right move for both of us.

Peyton Monroe just changed the game, and she doesn't even know it.

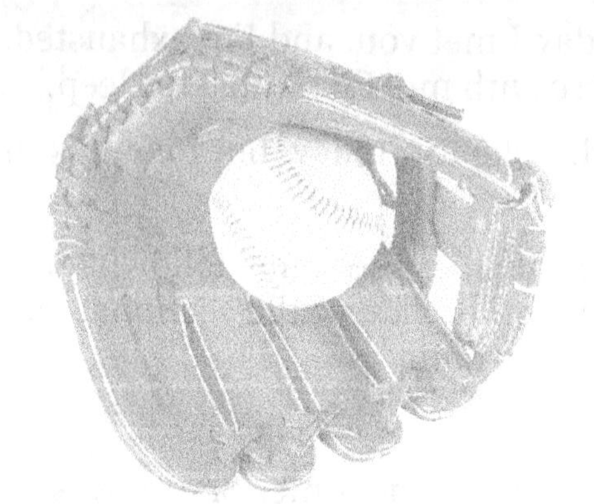

CHAPTER 9
Peyton

G RIFFIN IS HOLDING MY HAND tightly as he leads me into the kitchen. "There they are," his mom, Anna, smiles warmly.

"Sorry, we fell asleep." He stops next to the kitchen island, and to my surprise, he pulls me into his arms. "Dad, this is Peyton. Peyton, this is my dad, Gary."

"It's nice to meet you," I say respectfully, thrusting my hand over the kitchen island for him to shake. "Thank you for lunch, you didn't have to do that. It was delicious."

"It's nice to meet you as well, Peyton. We've heard a lot about you." He winks as he takes my hand in his. "And you're welcome. It was my pleasure. I'm glad that you and your family enjoyed it."

I turn to look at Griffin, and he shrugs. "I'm not denying it."

"All good, I hope," I reply.

"Most definitely," he assures me.

"It looks like you started without us," Griffin says, eyeing the perfectly grilled steaks on the counter.

"I came downstairs, and you were both conked out, and we were starving. I figured as long as the steak was tender enough to cut with a fork, you would be okay with it," his dad explains with a smile.

"I guess I'll just have to cook for you next time," Griffin says to me.

Next time. I have tonight and tomorrow with him, and after that, I don't know when the next time will be. That causes my chest to tighten. "Everything looks great. Thank you for having me," I say, pushing the words past the lump slowly forming in the back of my throat.

"Grab a plate," Gary says, pointing at the stack. "It's hot as hell outside, but we can eat out there or in here," he tells us.

"I vote for the air-conditioning," Griffin speaks up.

"Oh, thank God." Anna sighs, and we all laugh.

After filling our plates with steak, baked potatoes, and salad, we head to the dining room. "What do you want to drink?" Griffin asks. He rattles off a whole list of options.

"Lemonade, please."

"Coming right up." He bends to kiss the top of my head and leaves me alone with his mom while he goes to help his dad gather drinks.

"Wow." She smiles. "I've never seen him like this. It's nice," Anna confesses.

"Like what?" I have a pretty good idea of what she's going to say, but a part of me wants to hear her say it. Maybe I need it just as much as I want it. He's asking for more, and I'm still trying to decide whether we should try to make a go of this. I want to, but the distance holds me back.

"He's never brought a girl home. Not just for him, that is. We've had get-togethers, and some of his classmates and friends bring girls, but never Griffin. He's very... selective," she says with a smile.

"We have that in common. It's hard to find someone interested in me and not my family," I say as Griffin and his dad come back into the room.

"Your dad plays baseball professionally, right?" Anna asks.

"He did. He's retired now. However, my brother-in-law plays, and my middle sister, Parker, her future husband plays as well."

"Wow." She smiles. "You're definitely a baseball family."

"Peyton plays softball. Her sisters did too," Griffin says, cutting into his steak with his fork. "It's nice to talk to a girl who's not trying to seduce me and can actually hold a conversation. And it's mass bonus points that she knows the game." He turns to look at me and nods to his fork that's holding a piece of steak that he cut off with it. "You ready?" he asks.

Playfully, I roll my eyes and pick up my fork. I cut off a piece without a knife and hold it up to him. "Here goes nothing." I take the bite and chew. The flavor explodes on my tongue, and the meat is tender. "So good," I say, smiling. "That's a first for me. Usually, I feel like I'm chewing on a piece of rubber when I eat steak."

"You must not have a good steak house in Tennessee," Gary says.

"We do, but I stopped ordering it a long time ago. I always just order chicken," I confess.

"Now you've got us," Griffin says.

My heart smiles and weeps at the same time. I have him for the rest of today and tomorrow, but then what? How can the idea of leaving someone I've known a handful of days make my heart hurt the way that it does?

The rest of dinner goes smoothly. Griffin's parents are nice, and I can tell how close the three of them are by their teasing and banter. It reminds me of my family. It's growing every day, adding Cameron, Jett, and the new baby, as well as Holden. It's always a good time when we're together. I can see Griffin there with us. He's already proven he can fit in with our crowd.

Once my dad comes to terms with the fact that Griffin's in my life, I know he will love him too. Cam and Holden, and even Uncle Drew, took to him easily enough. Parker's on board. She texted me as soon as we left the restaurant, telling me he has her stamp of approval.

"Thank you for dinner," I tell them as Griffin and his dad stand to clear our plates. I stand to help him, but his mom waves for me to sit.

"You're our guest." She smiles kindly.

"It's the least I can do," I counter.

"Honey, they're just going to toss those into the dishwasher and call it a day." She laughs.

"What are you kids up to for the rest of the night?" Gary asks as he and Griffin step back into the dining room.

My eyes flash to Anna, and she nods, letting me know she was right, and I smile at her. "I have no idea," I confess, looking at Griffin for help.

"Movie?" he suggests.

"Sure."

"Well, we're going out," his dad announces.

"We are?" Anna asks, surprised.

"Yep. Marsha and Heath are going dancing, and I told them we'd go with them."

"And this is why I love you," Anna says, standing from her seat. "I'll be ready to go in ten," she says as she rushes out of the room, making us all laugh.

"Have fun," Griffin tells his dad. He stands and laces his fingers through mine and leads me downstairs to the basement.

"What do you want to watch?" he asks.

"I don't care." It's true. I don't care. I just want to spend time with him.

"How about we talk instead?"

"What do you want to talk about?" I ask, but I'm pretty certain I already know.

"Anything." He sits on the couch and pulls me down onto his lap.

"Why are you always pulling me onto your lap?"

"Does it bother you?"

"No. I was just curious."

"Honest answer? I'm not sure. I like having you close and touching you. I know that after tomorrow it's going to be a long time before I get to again, and I guess I'm just trying to soak up as much of you as I can get."

Neither one of us says anything for several long minutes. We're both content to just sit here and enjoy each other. My mind is flipping through every scenario of long distance, and even though I think it's doomed, I still want to try. I really like this guy.

"What's your favorite color?" he asks me.

"Blue. What's yours?"

"Blue." He grins. "Favorite food?"

"Lasagna. My mom makes it from scratch and it's so good," I tell him. "You?"

"Carbs." He chuckles. "I love it all. There's not much I won't eat."

"I hate onions."

"Good to know."

"When I was little, I would order onion rings when we would go out to eat. I'd peel the breading off and leave a pile of onions on my plate."

"So it's not the taste?"

"No, I think it's the texture. I just don't like them."

"Hobbies?" he asks.

"Softball, school, which isn't really much of a hobby as it is a necessity, hanging with Karina and our friends, spending time with my family. Especially my nephew, Jett. He's my older sister Paisley's son. He's so much fun to be around. She's pregnant again, and I can't wait to meet my new niece or nephew."

"That's something I won't have unless I marry someone who has siblings. That's the sucky part about being an only child."

"You have Oliver. He's your best friend. I can imagine his kids will be your nieces and nephews. Kind of like my uncle Drew. He's not my uncle by blood, but he is in my heart."

"I guess I never really thought about it like that."

"What about you? Hobbies?"

"Baseball, school, which like you said is a necessity, the guys, that's about all I have time for."

"All the more reason not to add a long-distance relationship that's sure to be stressful being away from each other to the list."

"You see, regardless of whether or not you agree to date me exclusively, you're still not going to be far from my mind." He places his hand on my jaw, and I turn my head to look him in the eye. "You're not easy to forget."

His whispered confession has the butterflies take flight once again. Who am I kidding? They never leave when he's around. I'm sitting sideways on his lap with my feet propped up on the couch. We're close, so close that I could lean in and kiss him. I want to, but I don't want to make the first move. I don't know why. It's not like there are written rules for these kinds of things. He's trying to get me to date him long-distance, or at least continue talking to see where things go. I know he wouldn't reject me, but I still don't want to make the first move. I don't have a ton of experience, and what if I mess up, or... gah, I need to just get out of my own head.

"Peyton?"

"Yeah," I say, shaking out of my thoughts.

"Can I kiss you?"

Is he a mind reader? "Please."

His hand slides behind my neck as he leans in close. Tentatively, he presses his lips to mine. They're softer than I imagined. It's just a quick brush of our lips, but it sends fire racing through my veins. I've never had that happen just from a kiss. Hell, I don't know if I've ever had that happen.

"Did you feel that?"

"Feel what?" I pretend I don't know what he's talking about. Maybe the earth didn't move for him like it did for me.

"Electricity."

Okay, then again, maybe he did. "I thought it was just me."

"Not just you. I think we should try that again, you know, just to be sure." The corner of his mouth lifts in a smile as he leans in again. This time, his tongue traces my lips, and they part automatically, welcoming him. The kiss is languid as he explores my mouth. One hand still rests on the back of my neck, while the other wraps around my waist, holding me close.

I lose all track of time as he kisses me. He's in no hurry as his tongue lazily strokes against mine. I try not to think about how much practice he's had at this very thing and more. I hate the thought of someone else getting this side of him. I can't control his past, but maybe just maybe, if I'm willing to take a leap of faith, I can control our future. It would take a lot of trust and communication. I'm not afraid to put in the work, but I don't know him well enough to know if the trust will be there. We haven't had enough time to build that foundation.

Griffin pulls away from the kiss and rests his forehead against mine. "What's going on inside that pretty head of yours?" he whispers.

"So many things, Griffin."

"Stand up for me," he says, dropping his hand that's resting behind my neck and tapping my thigh. I do as he says and watch as he moves to lie down on the couch, just like he did earlier today. He pats the spot in front of him. I move to lie down, and his words stop me. "Face me. I need to look into your eyes, and I'm not done kissing you."

Doing as he asks, I lie down, facing him. He wraps his arms around me and holds me close, and places a kiss on the top of my head.

"Talk."

"It's stupid."

"It's not stupid. If something is on your mind important enough to capture your thoughts, I want to hear it."

"It's embarrassing."

"Hey." His index finger rests under my chin, and he lifts my gaze to his. "There is nothing you can't tell me. You know what? I'll go first. I was thinking about how it's going to suck to go weeks, maybe even months at a time without kissing you."

"I was wondering how many girls you've snuck down here. How many you've kissed like you're kissing me." I pause. "And more," I confess.

"None. I've never brought a girl down here. I told you that I don't bring girls home. I've kissed my fair share and fooled around with a few, but none of them have been here, in my home. Only you."

This time, I initiate the kiss. I press my lips to his, and he tightens his hold on me. He gently strokes my back while the other hand tethers me to him. Once again, we get lost in the moment. My hand slides under his T-shirt and cautiously explores the dips and valleys of his abs. I lose myself in the moment in him. When his hands slide to the button of my blue jean shorts, I stiffen. He immediately stops and pulls his mouth from mine.

"I'm sorry, Peyton. I got carried away."

"It's not that," I rush to reassure him. "I just... I'm a virgin." I blurt the words out. Just like pulling off a Band-Aid, I need to get it out there so he knows exactly what he's getting into, or what he's not, I guess I should say. I bury my face in his chest to hide my embarrassment. I know there is nothing to be embarrassed about, but the heat coats my cheeks all the same.

Both of his arms wrap around me, and he pulls me close. Our bodies are aligned, and I can feel his hard length pressed against me. He's going to think I'm some kind of tease. I hate these kinds of situations.

"Peyton?" he says softly.

I don't answer. I don't even acknowledge him from where my head is buried in his chest.

"Come on, beautiful, please look at me."

There's something in his voice. I can't quite explain it. It's filled with understanding and something I can't name, but whatever it is, it gives me the courage to lift my head and look at him.

"Me too," he confesses softly.

"You too what?"

"I'm a virgin, Peyton."

"What? No. No way." I lean back to get a better look at his face. His eyes are staring into mine, and I don't see an ounce of deceit in them.

"I am." He pulls me back into his chest, and I go willingly as I process this news. "Remember when I mentioned my baseball coach was big on telling us to wrap it before we tap it. And yes, that's exactly how he would word it. He went on to explain that those with talent tend to attract those who want a meal ticket or want to ride the coattails of fame and fortune. He put fear in us. He told us all kinds of stories about players getting piss-ass drunk and girls taking advantage of them trying to get pregnant. He told us to never let the woman provide the protection, that she could poke holes in the condom or lie about birth control."

"Someone hurt him."

"Probably. Looking back, I'd say you're right. At the time, we all just took it as a coach looking out for us. I told you about Jack getting that girl pregnant during our sophomore year in high school. After that, it just wasn't worth it to me."

"You were lucky. That he was looking out for all of you."

"Yeah, I guess we were."

"They do the same thing in the majors. I'm not sure if it's the head coach, but they go to training for this kind of thing. I know my dad had to do it, and I've heard Cameron and Holden talk about it as well."

"Yet some still fall victim."

"There's one in every crowd," I say, lightening the mood.

"Are you waiting? For marriage?" he adds.

"Are you?"

He chuckles. "No. Not really. I've just never found someone who I trust is here for me and not what I can do for them. Not until I found you, that is."

"I'm not either. I'm in the same boat. So many know who I am in our hometown, and they want to get closer to the game, my dad, my uncle, and my brothers-in-law. I'm including Holden in that," I explain. "He might as well be married to my sister. He loves her fiercely."

"We're more alike than you thought, huh," he asks.

"We are."

"Stay with me."

"What do you mean? I have to go home, Griffin. My family is there. I have school and the team."

"Tonight. Stay with me tonight."

"Your parents?"

"They know how much I like you. Besides, we're both adults."

"I'm not having sex with you."

"I didn't ask you to," he counters. "What I am asking is for you to stay with me. I'm not ready for this night to end. I have tomorrow, and then I don't know how long it will be before I can see you again. I just really want to hold you. I want to know for the first time in my life what it's like to sleep with a woman in my arms and wake up with her the same way."

"That's hard to say no to."

"Then say yes."

"I'll need to call Parker. Let her know I'm not coming back tonight."

"Where's your phone?" he asks.

"On the table." I turn and grab it, almost falling off the couch in the process. My hands shake as I pull up Parker's contact.

"Hey, if this makes you uncomfortable, you don't have to. I'll take you home," he says, placing his hand over mine.

"No. It's not that. It's just... a first for me too."

"Good." He kisses me quickly.

I hit send on Parker's name and place the phone next to my ear. I could have texted her, but I know my sister. She would have called wanting to hear my voice to make sure that I'm okay.

"How was the steak?" she asks.

"So good. I was able to cut it with a fork," I tell her. Griffin smiles and points at himself, causing me to shake my head at his antics. He didn't do the cooking, but I have no doubt that the results would be the same. He learned from one of the best. "Hey, I wanted to tell you that I'm not coming back to the room tonight. I'm going to stay here. With Griffin."

"Do you have protection?" she asks.

"I don't need it."

"Peyton—" she starts.

"I'm not going to need it, Parker. Trust me."

"Okay. If you need me at any time, you call me. Understand? I can be there in ten minutes."

"I'll be fine, but thank you."

"I love you, lady," she says with laughter in her voice.

"I love you too, duchess," I reply, then end the call. I place my phone on the floor and turn back to Griffin.

"I still think your dad is a genius." He grins.

"Make sure you tell him that if you ever meet him. That will give you brownie points."

"I'm going to meet him, Peyton. We're going to make this work."

"I want it to," I confess.

"Thank fuck," he says, kissing the corner of my mouth. "That's the first time you've let me know what you were thinking about this. About us."

"It all seems too good to be true."

"If we both want it… if we're both willing to sacrifice and put in the work, we can do it."

"You miss one hundred percent of the shots you never take," I say.

"And we're taking ours," he says, pressing his lips to mine.

CHAPTER 10
Griffin

I DON'T KNOW WHAT TIME it is. The house above us is quiet, and Peyton is sleeping peacefully in my arms. We kissed for hours. So long that I lost track of time. My lips are sore, and hers are red and swollen. We talked some more about life, and dreams, and family. You name it, we've talked about it.

The more I get to know her, the more this idea takes root inside my chest.

I know that we can do this.

It's going to suck hairy monkey balls. Being without her and not having nights like last night will be hard when all I want is to be near her. I'm already running through my schedule in my mind and calculating the first chance I might have to go to Tennessee to see her.

She leaves tomorrow, and if you would have told me I'd be torn up about that after only knowing her a handful of days, I'd tell you that you'd lost your damn mind, but here we are. Emotion wells in my throat just thinking about her stepping onto the plane and flying home.

I sent my dad a text and told him she was staying and that we were down here. He asked me if I needed protection. Peyton and I laughed about that, considering her sister asked us the same thing. It's not that I don't want to, but we have a hard road ahead of us. We need to build more trust. I need to be able to prove to her that this is going to work before we go there.

I'm tired as hell. I've barely slept since I met her. We napped earlier, but I can't seem to fall asleep. Not when I know it's going to be a long damn time before I'm back in this place with her.

"Why are you awake?" her sleep-laced voice asks.

I hold her a little tighter and press my lips to her forehead. "Just thinking."

"Want to talk about it?"

"I'm going to miss the hell out of you."

"This is going to be hard, Griffin."

"Nothing worth having comes easy. It's going to be more than hard. It's going to suck. I'm afraid to close my eyes and miss a single second of time with you."

"You can't be sleep-deprived. Tomorrow is my last day. I need you rested."

"Oh, yeah? What are we going to do exactly?"

"I want to go back to the beach. It's my last day here. I'd like to soak up some sun."

"Then that's what we'll do."

She snuggles a little closer. "I'll be here when you wake up, Griff. I promise."

My heart hammers in my chest. "Okay."

"Please get some rest. I'm right here," she says, placing a kiss on my chest.

"Where you belong," I say, closing my eyes. Maybe I just needed her reassurance that she'd still be here because it doesn't take long for sleep to finally claim me.

"Hello?" I hear the sweetest voice say. "No, I'm at Griffin's." She pauses. "I stayed here last night." Another pause. "No, we didn't do that," she says, her voice a rushed whisper. "It was nice." Another pause. "Yeah, I told Griffin that I want to go to the beach today. He's still sleeping. I'll text you when we're up and moving." Another shorter pause. "We can talk about this later," she says, her voice low. "I'll text you. Bye," she says, ending the call.

"Karina?" I ask, making her jump.

"You scared me." She places her phone back on the floor and rolls over to snuggle into me. Sometime during the night, one of us must have pulled the blanket from the back of the couch and covered us. "Yeah, that was Karina. She wanted to know what we were doing today."

"You and me? Or you and her?"

"All of us, if that's okay."

"I don't care who is there as long as I'm with you."

"You're sweet in the mornings."

"I'm always sweet," I counter, tugging the cover over us.

"Yeah, you kind of are."

"Only with you, though."

"I don't know. I saw you with your mom."

"Yeah, the two most important women in my life." As soon as she agreed to see where this goes, even after she leaves tomorrow, I decided I was no longer going to hide how I felt about her. Hell, I haven't really been hiding it at all. But communication will be the key to making this work, and I never want to doubt for a second that she's all that I can see. It took one look to know she was special, but after spending time with her, I know without a shadow of a doubt that she's unlike anyone I've ever met. There will only ever be one Peyton Monroe.

"Those are big words, Griffin Anthony."

"These are big feelings, Peyton Monroe."

"Go shower, so you can take me to my hotel, and I can do the same. The beach and sunshine are calling my name."

"So bossy," I tease. Leaning in, I press my lips to hers. When I slide my tongue across her lips, she refuses to open it. I pull back and study her. "What's wrong?"

She places her hand over her mouth. "I need to brush my teeth."

"Baby, that's not going to stop me. I have less than twenty-four hours left with you." I lean in and kiss her again, but she still refuses to open. This won't do. Climbing over her, I stand from the couch, stretch and lift her into my arms, bridal style.

"What are you doing?" She laughs.

"I want my good morning kiss." That's the only explanation I give her as I carry her upstairs and then up another flight to my room.

"Your parents," she hisses.

"They've both gone to work. It's just you and me," I say, swatting her ass lightly. She giggles, and my smile widens. She's happy. Now all I have to do is figure out how to keep that up while we're hundreds of miles away from each other.

Once in my room, I carry her to my attached bathroom and set her on the counter. Reaching under the cabinet, I pull out a new toothbrush and hand it to her. "Chop chop," I say, reaching for my own toothbrush and the tube of toothpaste that's on the counter.

"Now, who's bossy?" she asks.

"I'm going to brush my teeth, and as soon as I'm done, I'm claiming my good morning kiss. You better get to it," I say, placing a glob of toothpaste onto my brush, running it under some water, and sticking it in my mouth. I watch her as she giggles but does the same thing.

I spit, and use my hand like a cup and rinse my mouth. She does the same, and I don't even let her wipe her mouth off with the towel before my lips crash against hers. This time, she opens for me. She moans as she wraps her legs around my waist and her arms around my neck.

My cock is nestled between her thighs, and I can't help but notice that this is the perfect angle and position. If we were naked, I could slide into her heat and feel her warmth on my cock. I can't tell you how many times I've thought about sex. A few girls have had me so worked up that I contemplated maybe taking things further, but I always backed off. That trust just wasn't there.

With Peyton, I wouldn't have an ounce of hesitation. If she was ready, if *we* were ready, I would make her mine. My cock twitches just thinking about it.

"You're, uh..." She pulls back and looks down where I'm pressing against her pussy. "We should probably stop. I'm sorry, I didn't mean to." She drops her legs, but I capture them, bringing them back around my waist.

"Never apologize for kissing me, Peyton."

"But you're... uncomfortable."

"Nothing Rosey can't fix," I tell her.

She stiffens, and I realize my mistake.

I lift my hand and grin. "Peyton, meet Rosey palm. She and my cock are very well acquainted."

Her mouth drops open, and then she's laughing. We're talking hysterical, head-tilted back, belly laughing. "Oh my God."

"No other woman in my life but you, Peyton. I know it's going to take time for us to build that trust, but I'm telling you there is no one but you."

"I only want you."

"You want me, huh?"

"Yeah, I… yes."

"Are you wet for me?" I bend my knees to look at her in the eye.

"Stop. It's embarrassing."

"Fuck that. It's not embarrassing. It's hot as fuck. You need me to take care of you?" In my head, I'm begging her to say yes.

"What about you?"

"I asked first."

"You can if I can."

Fuck me.

My hands rest on either side of her face, and I make sure I have her full attention. "Tell me what you want, Peyton."

"I want to take care of this," she says, running her fingers over the crotch of my shorts.

"You first. Tell me," I urge her.

"Don't make me say it."

"Hey." I bend my knees again so we are eye to eye. "It's just me. We're about to embark on a crazy-as-fuck adventure of dating, living states away from each other. Communication is going to be key for us. Never be ashamed or embarrassed about what you want or how you feel. Not with me, Peyton. Never with me."

"What if I told you that I want you to fuck me?" Her cheeks are bright red.

"I'd take you to my bed and give you what you want."

"Griffin," she breathes.

"I know it's you. I can't explain it, but I know it deep in my gut. So if you want me to fuck you, I'll do it."

"I-I'm not there yet."

"Then tell me what you want."

"Your hands, and maybe… maybe your mouth."

"Maybe?"

"Only if you want. I don't know if all guys like that sort of thing, and I've never, so… never mind. Just forget I said it."

"No." No fucking way can I forget that she said that. I'm going to give her what she wants. Picking her up in my arms, I carry her to my bed. Setting her down gently on the mattress, I move to the door and shut and lock it just in case my parents do happen to come home while we're here. Walking back to the bed, I watch her intently as she stares at me. Her chest is rising and falling with rapid breaths, and she's squeezing her hands into fists.

"You're in charge here, Peyton. You say when, how, stop. You hold all the control."

She nods. "Okay."

I strip out of my clothes. I can't let her leave tomorrow without knowing what it feels like to have her skin to skin. This memory will have to hold me over until I can see her again. I grip my cock and stroke it a few times, her eyes following the movement of my hand.

She moves to climb off the bed, and when she lifts her shirt over her head, tossing it on the floor, I stroke faster. My eyes follow her every movement as she undresses until she's standing before me, completely naked.

"You're beautiful."

"So are you." She bites down on her bottom lip.

"Back in bed." My tone is commanding, but I have to be. I'm ready to lose my shit. I've seen naked women. I've done my fair share of messing around, but none of them holds a candle to the beauty before me.

She climbs into bed and slides under the covers, holding them up for me. I slide in next to her and pull her close. "Damn," I mutter when she wraps her arms around me. "I don't know how I'm going to let you get on that plane tomorrow," I confess.

"Shh... let's not talk about that right now. Let's just be."

"I can do that," I say as my hand ventures to her pussy. I stroke her clit with my thumb. Her head falls back to the pillow, and she closes her eyes. I trace my finger through her folds, feeling her wetness coat my hand before sliding in one long digit. My mouth wraps around one rosebud nipple as I suck gently.

"Oh," she breathes, her eyes still closed.

"Peyton, open your eyes for me." Her eyes pop open. "I need you to keep them on me, okay?" Her brows furrow as I slide in another digit. "I just... need your eyes on me." I can't explain my reaction to her. I never gave a fuck if the girl was watching. As long as it appeared like she was getting off, I was fine with it, but not with Peyton. I need her to know that it's me. I need to know that she's aware that I'm giving her the pleasure her body yearns for.

Only me.

I lazily pump my fingers in and out. I'm in no rush. Hell, I could lie here all damn day, just like this.

"Griff?"

"Tell me what you need."

"Kiss me."

I do what she asks, kissing her slow and deep. "Close," she pants against my mouth.

I remove my fingers and bring them to my mouth, tasting her. She whines in protest, but I'm not going to leave her hanging. Tossing the covers over my head, I move down her body to settle between her thighs. My fingers find their home inside her pussy, while my mouth finds her clit.

Her hands bury in my hair, and she lifts her hips. The action only spurs me on. I suck on her clit, then massage it with my tongue, alternating the motions while my fingers pump steadily in and out of her. I feel her walls start to tighten, and I know she's there. I don't stop until she cries out my name, and her grip on my hair relaxes.

Kissing my way back up her body, I pop my head out from underneath the covers. "So sweet," I murmur, pressing my lips to hers. She doesn't protest. Instead, she rolls to her side and pushes me to my back.

This time it's her head that's disappearing under the covers and her silky soft hands that grip my cock. I toss the covers back so I can watch the show. It's not one I want to miss, and I decide I should warn her.

"I'm already close," I say huskily.

Her reply is to bend her head and wrap her lips around my cock. I grip the sheets to keep from tightening her hair around my fist and assisting her. She's doing just fine on her own. Over and over and over again, her head bobs up and down, taking my cock in her mouth. My eyes threaten to roll back in my head, but I force myself to keep them open. I don't want to miss a single second of this.

When she peers up at me under her lashes, that does it. "Peyton." I tap her shoulder. "I'm gonna come." My voice is strangled. She doesn't move. Instead, she increases her efforts, her head bobbing faster, her hands pumping in tandem with her mouth. "Tell me—" I stop and take a deep breath. "Tell me where you want me to come," I plead. She doesn't answer, and I'm too far gone to ask again. My orgasm tears through me like lightning, and she takes it all. She swallows every last drop, releases me with an audible pop, and moves back up to lie next to me.

Grabbing the covers, I manage to pull them over us and tug her to my chest. "Fuck," I say, kissing the top of her head.

"Was that okay? I've never... I mean hand jobs, but never that."

"You blew my mind," I assure her.

"It wasn't as nasty as I thought it would be," she says, making me laugh.

"You didn't have to do that," I remind her even though the act is already done.

"If I was going to try it, I wanted it to be with you."

"I wish you could stay."

"We're not talking about that. Now, go shower so we can head to my hotel."

"Come with me?"

"Tempting, but no. I don't trust myself."

"I'll be good. I promise."

"It's not you I'm worried about. I seem to let down all my defenses where you're concerned."

"Good. I want inside the walls you've built here." I tap her chest over her heart.

"Go. Shower. I need a shower and some food and the beach. In that order."

"You want to clean up first?" I offer.

"Yes. Actually, that's a better idea." She kisses me quickly and climbs over the top of me and out of my bed. I watch as she gathers her clothes and scurries to the bathroom. When the door closes behind her, I stare up at the ceiling and process what just happened. Grabbing my phone, I start looking at my baseball schedule and the possible times to go see her. I don't know how I'm going to survive this. I just know that I have to. I can't let her go.

CHAPTER 11
Peyton

TODAY HAS BEEN INCREDIBLE. AFTER we both showered, him at his place and me at the hotel, we went to the hotel restaurant for lunch. The guys and Karina joined us, and the entire time, Griffin had his hands on me. His arm around my shoulders, his hand on my thigh, his lips brushing my temple, and holding my hand. His friends raised their eyebrows but didn't comment. Not that it would have mattered. We're on borrowed time, and neither one of us was willing to let an opportunity to touch the other pass us by.

"Yo, Griff, let's do this," Sam calls out.

"It's dark!" Griffin calls back.

"That makes it more fun. We have the light of the fire," Ollie points out.

"I'm good," he says.

We're currently sitting on a towel spread out on the sand next to the fire. I'm sitting between his legs, his arms wrapped around me, and Karina is on her towel a few feet away. "You should go." I turn to look at him over my shoulder.

"No." He tightens his hold on me.

"I'm not going to disappear," I tease.

"Not funny, Peyton. You leave in twelve hours."

Picking up my phone, I see that it's just after nine, and my flight leaves at nine in the morning.

"You can't ignore your friends when I'm around. They'll hate me."

"No, they won't. They know you're leaving." He buries his face in my neck. "I can't do it, Peyton, so don't ask me to. I can't leave your side right now."

Karina points at us. "I'm loving this," she says as she stands. "I'll be your fourth," she calls out to Sam.

I watch her as she jogs off to play Frisbee in the dark of night.

"I'm sorry."

"For what?"

"Keeping you from your friends."

"You're not. I'm making a choice to hold my girlfriend for as long as I can."

My heart stutters in my chest. "Is that what I am? Your girlfriend?"

"I thought we went over this?"

"We said that we were going to try. We said that we would see if we could make a go of a long-distance relationship. We didn't really label it."

"Let's label it. I'm not letting you get on the plane tomorrow without knowing that you're mine, Peyton. I can't do it," he says, his voice grave.

I don't even have to think about it. Not after this morning. "I'm yours."

"Thank fuck," he mutters, kissing my neck. "I was looking at my schedule earlier. I was trying to find a time when I had two or three days with no games and hopefully no practice so that I can come and see you."

"Did you have any luck?"

"I think so. I'll have to wait and see if Coach adds any practices to our schedule."

I'm quiet while I think about my own schedule and if I'll be able to hop on a quick flight to come and see him. "When's your birthday?" I ask.

"November. When's yours?"

"April."

"You'll be nineteen?" he asks.

"Yeah. You too?"

"Twenty. My birthday was late in the year, so I was almost six when I started kindergarten."

"Damn, and here I thought I could tease you about dating an older woman," I joke.

Music begins to play from a speaker that's perched on a cooler. It's a fast country song, and I know that we've line danced to it at a frat party earlier this year. One song bleeds into another until a slow one comes on.

"Dance with me?" he whispers in my ear. He doesn't let me answer before he's climbing to his feet and pulling me with him. He wraps me in his arms, and I rest my head against his chest. I can feel the heavy rhythm of his heartbeat. He holds me as if I'm the most precious thing in his world, and it brings tears to my eyes. I can't believe I came to Florida for spring break and ended up falling for this guy. Not only that, he's my boyfriend, and we live almost thirteen hours away from each other.

When "10,000 Hours" begins to play, he softly sings the lyrics to me. We're barely swaying by the time the song ends, and there are tears in my eyes and a lump in my throat.

"I never knew I could feel like this. I didn't know I could fall for someone so quickly," he tells me.

"I feel it too."

"We're going to make this happen, Peyton. I promise you we will."

"Come on," I tell him. "Your friends are missing you."

"I see them every day. My time with you is dwindling fast." We make it to the fire, and Karina is folding up her towel.

"Hey, I'm drained," she tells us. "Oliver said he would walk me back to the hotel."

"We're going too," Griffin answers. We hadn't talked about that, but I know we're both on edge with the time of my flight getting closer and closer.

I squeeze his hand, and he looks down at me, giving me his full attention. "I'm not ready to leave you," I say in a hushed voice.

"I'm not leaving. I'm staying with you tonight."

"You are?"

"Yeah, I already told Parker and Holden."

"When?"

"When you were in the shower earlier."

"What did you say?" I can only imagine the conversation and how it went over.

"I told them that you mean a lot to me and that it's killing me that you're leaving in the morning. I told them I wasn't willing to be away from you until the minute I had to. I hate to leave you at security at the airport and that it would be easier on you if we stayed there, but if they were against that, we would stay at my place again."

"Oh my God! You did not."

He turns his back to our friends and lifts my chin. "I did. I told you. I'm not leaving you until I absolutely have to."

"What did they say?"

"Parker teared up and nodded her agreement. Holden shook my hand, and that was it."

"You're staying with me?" Hot tears prick my eyes.

"I'm staying with you. And I'm driving you to the airport, and I'm not leaving your side until I have to. I almost bought a ticket just so that I could sit with you while you wait for your flight."

"That's crazy."

"I know. The flight was sold out."

"Griffin!"

He winks and turns back to our friends. "I'll catch you guys later."

"You going to be home later?" Oliver asks him.

"No. I'm staying with my girl. I'll be around tomorrow after I get home from the airport." My belly flops when he calls me his girl. "Ready?" he asks.

"I need to get my towel."

He drops my hand and makes quick work of picking up the towel and shaking out the sand before folding it and coming back to me. He laces his fingers through mine and nods at Oliver, and then we're walking. The four of us make the trek back up the beach to our hotel. Oliver and Karina chat back and forth, but Griffin and I are both quiet.

"You need a ride tomorrow?" Oliver asks Griffin.

"Nah, I have my Jeep here. Thanks, though."

"Hit me up tomorrow when you get back." He leans in and hugs Karina, whispering something in her ear that makes her laugh before she swats at his arm as he steps back from her.

"Have a safe flight." Karina gives me a hug, then turns to face Griffin. "If you hurt her, I'll fly here and rip your balls off." She's dead serious, not a glimmer of a smile anywhere in her expression. My best friend is fiercely loyal.

We step onto the elevator, and Griffin turns to face her, his hand still holding tightly to mine.

"I don't want to hurt her, Karina. I'd hurt myself before that happened."

"How about neither of you gets hurt? I like what's behind door number three much better, don't you?" She finally lets her grin tilt her lips.

"Done."

"I'll call you when I land," Karina tells me as the door slides open, dropping her off at her floor. She waves as the doors close, and it's just the two of us.

When we reach our floor, we step out of the elevator together. My hands shake as I tap our key card on the door, and the light flashes green. The room is dark and quiet. Parker's bedroom door is open, so I know she's not here. Without a word, I lead Griffin into my room, then close and lock the door behind us.

Wordlessly, we both strip out of our clothes and climb under the covers. We lie facing each other without a sliver of room between our naked bodies. I want to tell him that I'm falling hard, but it's too soon for that. Instead, I rest my head on his chest and listen to the rhythm of his thundering heartbeat.

"Call me every day," he says, his voice cracking. "Text me whenever you want. If I'm at practice or a game, I'll get back to you as soon as I can. I want to know everything that happens in your life. I want you to call and text me so much that I feel like I'm there. I don't want to miss a single thing."

"W-Will you do the same?"

"Yes."

"And we can video call, right?"

"We can. We'll have to sit down one night to figure out our schedules and plan times to video call. And I want to come and see you as soon as I can get away."

"I can come back too. If I have a break."

"We're going to make this work, Peyton. There is no other option."

"There is. Maybe it wasn't meant to be."

He stiffens. "I've waited all this time for you, so no way in hell am I letting you slip through my fingers. I'm not afraid of the work. I'm a D1 college athlete with a double major. Work is my middle name."

"That's different. Those are your hopes and dreams. Your goals for life."

"And this is my heart. You are my heart."

I suck in a breath. "Griffin..." His name is a whispered plea.

"You're my girl, and as time passes and we grow closer, I know there is no way my heart won't be invested," he explains. "I'm not so sure it's not already," he adds quietly.

"I guess I should get some sleep. I still have to pack in the morning. It's just... I don't know if I can. Sleep, I mean."

"Yeah, I don't think sleep is in the cards for me tonight."

"Tell me about you. Tell me everything. We have all night."

"You willing to do the same?" he asks.

"Detail for detail," I answer.

That's how we spend the next several hours—talking about our childhoods, our love of sports and music. We talk more about food and family traditions for birthdays and holidays. We talk about so much that by the time four o'clock rolls around, I feel as if I've known him for years.

"You need to get some rest," he says.

"I've always wondered what it felt like."

"What's that?" he asks, rubbing his hand up and down my spine.

"To lie skin to skin with someone."

"It's better than I imagined," he replies. "Then again, maybe it's the someone who makes all the difference."

"You're definitely my someone."

"Get some rest," he says. I feel his lips press to the top of my head.

Although I want to fight it, we both need to sleep. As it stands, it's already only going to be a few short hours. I close my eyes, and the exhaustion weighs heavily as I start to drift off to sleep. It's Griffin's, "Fuck, I'm going to miss you," and his soothing touch that lulls me to sleep.

I don't want to do this.

We're standing just inside the airport, my suitcase at my side and Griffin at the other. My sister said goodbye to Holden at the hotel to avoid the media circus that was sure to follow him. She's standing off to the side, giving us time.

"I need to go." The words taste sour on my tongue.

"I know," he says, his chin resting on top of my head. "I know you do, but I don't want to let go."

"You have to."

"I don't know how this happened, Peyton. I don't know how I got attached to you in such a short amount of time, but I feel like someone is reaching into my chest and yanking out my heart."

"We don't have to do this. If it's too hard, we can step back from all of it."

"Fuck that." He pulls back and bends his knees so we are eye to eye. "I'm not backing away from you. Not now, and probably not ever. It's going to be hard, and it's going to suck, but I know we can do this. I know we can."

"Okay."

"Tell me you know we can do this, Peyton."

"We can do this." I say the words, but I'm not so sure that they're true. I want to believe that we can, but I know we're young, and distance is hard.

"I miss you already." He rests his forehead against mine.

"I have to go."

"Come on." He pulls away, but I stop him.

"We should part ways here."

"What? No. I can walk with you to security."

"It's going to hurt no matter where we say goodbye, Griffin."

He nods, a solemn look on his face. "Then I better make this good," he says, pulling me behind a small pillar. "It's going to be a while before I get to kiss these lips." Bending, he places his hands on the back of my thighs and lifts me. On instinct, I wrap my arms and legs around him as his lips find mine.

I expect the kiss to be urgent, but he takes his time. Seconds bleed into minutes, and I know we have to stop. "Griff," I say against his lips.

"I know," he says, hugging me. "I know you have to go, and I hate it." He kisses me one last time, this one just a simple press of his lips to mine before he lowers my feet to the ground.

"If it's meant to be, it will be," I tell him.

"You can't talk like that. You have to stay positive. We are meant to be, and we will be," he counters with a small tilt to his lips. "Come on. I'll walk you back to Parker."

When we reach my sister, she gives me a sad, knowing smile. She knows what I'm feeling. She's leaving her boyfriend here as well. Relationships are hard, but if both parties put in the work, it can happen. I know this. I grew up a witness to this very thing.

"We've got this," I tell Griffin.

"There's my girl." He kisses me one last time before pulling away and hugging my sister. "Call me when you land," he says, stepping back.

"Definitely."

"Okay. I'm going to turn around now. I need you to start walking away. When I do it, I might not ever leave."

"I'll see you soon," I tell him.

He points at me and grins. "That. I'll see you soon." He turns and, without looking back, begins to walk away.

"Come on. Let's get moving. He's right. If we don't, it's just going to prolong it and make it worse."

Together, we make our way through the airport and through security. By the time we reach our gate, tears well in my eyes. I swallow them back and take a few deep breaths before I turn to face my sister. "Thank you, Parker. You convinced Dad to let me come with you, and I would never have met him otherwise."

"You're welcome," she says, putting her arm around my shoulders and hugging me close. "Griffin seems like a good guy."

"Yeah," I agree. He's a good guy who somehow managed to capture my heart in a matter of days.

CHAPTER 12
Griffin

I T'S BEEN A WEEK SINCE she's been gone. A week of calls and text messages. A week of missing her like crazy. This is going to be harder than I first thought. Not because I can't stay faithful, but missing her is torture. There is an ache in my chest, a hollow hole that can only be filled by her presence.

I hate it.

But I want her. All I have to do is remind myself that she's the prize in all of this, and my gut settles. We knew this was going to be hard. We knew this was going to be a challenge. I just didn't realize it would feel like this. Like a piece of me is missing.

"You want to head over to my place?" Oliver asks.

We just wrapped up practice, which means we're done for the day. All of our classes are early mornings to save time for games or practices in the evenings. "Yeah, but we need to stop to grab something to eat. I'm starving."

"That's the only thing I hate about moving back to campus—missing Mom's cooking," Oliver comments.

"Right? This makes me sound like a dick but come on. My dad's a chef. I'm a food snob." I shrug, and he laughs.

"How about the deli just outside of campus?"

"My mouth is watering just thinking about their roast beef sub. I'm in." We quickly gather our bags and head to the parking lot. Being roommates, we often ride together, and today was my day to drive.

"Have you talked to Peyton today?" he asks once we're in my Jeep and on the road.

"Yeah. Every morning."

"Look at you and that goofy-ass grin. I was sure it would have worn off by now."

"Why?" I laugh.

"Because she's there, and you're here."

"Yeah, that's hard, but I have to stay positive about this."

"You really like this girl, don't you?"

"Do you think I'd put myself through this if I didn't?" Oliver knows me better than that. I'm not sure where this conversation is going.

"No."

"Spit it out, man. What's on your mind?" Oliver and I have been best friends for longer than I can remember. Long before either of us really understood exactly what a best friend was. He's like a brother to me.

"Nothing."

"Try again," I tell him.

"I'm envious of you."

"Really?"

"Yeah. Peyton's great. I mean, I didn't get to spend a ton of time with her while she was here, but I can see how happy she makes you even living states away. I can't help but think that would be nice, you know?"

"You'll find her when you least expect her," I tell him. "I didn't expect Peyton, yet here I am."

"We're young."

"Doesn't mean my heart doesn't work." I laugh.

"Is your heart involved?"

I nod. "Yeah. My heart's involved."

"Are you in love with her?" he asks, shock evident in his tone.

"No, but I'm falling hard and fast," I confess. "I wish I could explain it to you, but it doesn't even make sense to me."

"Try," he urges.

I open my mouth to attempt to tell him how it feels to be with her. To know that she's in this with me, but my phone rings. I glance at the dash of my Jeep, and my smile widens. Reaching out, I tap the screen. "Hey," I greet my girl. "You're on speaker. Ollie and I are headed to grab some lunch."

"Hey, you. Hi, Oliver," she says.

"Hey, Peyton."

"How was practice?" she asks.

"Grueling. Yours?"

"About the same," she groans. "Took a ball to the shoulder."

"Shit."

"Yeah. I'm heading back to my apartment now. I'm going to ice it and just chill. I'm done for the day."

"I—" I start, but she stops me.

"I know, Griff. I'm fine. I promise. You two enjoy your lunch. I just wanted to check in."

"I'll call you when we get back to the dorm."

"Okay. Bye, Oliver."

"Bye, Peyton. Take care of that arm," he tells her.

"I'm on it." Her laughter dies off as she ends the call.

Frustrated, I run my hands through my hair. I hate that she's there and hurting, and I can't be there. I know there is nothing that I can do, but I could hold her. I could get her ice and sit with her.

"It's killing you, isn't it?" Oliver asks.

"What?"

"It's killing you that you can't be there with her."

"Is it that obvious?"

"It is."

"It's the 'her hurting' part that gets me. I wish I could be there."

"You know these kinds of injuries. There's nothing you could do to help her."

"No, but holding her would help me." That's the heart of the matter. I've never met a girl I just wanted to be there for. I'd give anything to be able to hold her right now. Take care of her as we lie around watching movies and icing her arm. It sounds like the perfect afternoon to me. Aside from her injury, I'd be there to take care of her.

"You're not falling, brother. You're already there."

"What?" I glance over at him as I pull into the lot of the deli. "I'm pretty sure I'd know if I was in love with her."

Oliver just shakes his head. "Come on. Let's get some lunch so we can get back to the dorm and you can call and check on her."

"You're talking my language," I tell him.

"Two weeks and your language is Peyton."

I don't argue the fact because it's true. "My chest is tight, and there's this happy, bubbly part of me that wants to shout to the world that she's mine. I miss her, but at the same time, I know she's doing something she loves. Long distance is harder than I thought it would be. I knew I would miss her, but it's been a week, and it feels like a part of me is missing."

"And you say you're not in love with her."

"I said I was falling."

"You've already crashed and burned," he jokes.

"Maybe." I shrug. "I can tell you that even though this sucks, the alternative is not having her in my life, and that's not something I'm willing to accept." I grab the keys from the ignition and climb out of the Jeep.

We're quiet as we walk into the deli. Girls call out to us. I wave, but I don't smile or flirt like I would have before. They're not Peyton, and none of them ever will be. We order our food and find a table. We're both diving in starving when two girls approach our table. One lays her hand on my shoulder, and the other does the same to Oliver. It's nothing new, but it feels different. Wrong even.

"Sorry." I turn to look at the girl. "Can you move your hand?"

"Oh." She looks taken aback that I would even ask. "I guess I could sit on your lap," she coos.

I don't bother holding the eye roll. "I have a girlfriend."

"Since when? Word on campus is you're single."

"Well, the word is wrong. I'm taken, so step back." I glance across the table at Oliver, and he barely contains his laughter.

"You don't have to be a dick about it," the girl seethes.

"Then stop touching me." I shift in my seat, and her hands drop from my arm.

"Whatever." She crosses her arms over her chest and storms off, her friend following hot on her heels.

"Sorry I fucked that up for you," I tell Oliver.

"Nah, I'm not interested."

"Since when?" I ask him. "Before I met Peyton, we would have been flirting our asses off with the two of them."

"Yeah, but that was pre-Peyton."

"I'm the one in a relationship, man. Not you."

"I told you I'm envious."

"Maybe she was the one?"

"No." He takes a long pull of his drink. "She's not the one. I want someone who I meet organically. You know, like my Frisbee landing at her feet on a random day at the beach with my friends. Those two saw us, knew we were athletes, and pounced. You've got me seeing things a little differently."

"Oh, yeah? Care to enlighten me?"

"I want a Peyton."

I point at him. "You can't have mine." I know he'd never, but I'm drawing clear lines in the sand with anyone and everyone when it comes to her.

Oliver tosses his head back in laughter. "Not yours, but someone like her. Someone real."

"Karina?"

He looks away. "She's chill and beautiful."

"Daniel?"

"She was passing through for him."

"And for you?"

"I can't stop thinking about her."

"So you coming with me when I go see Peyton?"

"When?"

"I don't know yet, but you can guarantee I'm going to figure it out. Soon."

"Count me in. We have to use our trust funds for something, right?" he asks.

Oliver and I both got trust funds from our grandparents when we turned eighteen. It's not millions, but it's enough for me to travel to see my girlfriend whenever I find the time in my schedule. Gramps told me not to blow it. To save it for something important, something that I loved. I smile to myself. I'll have to call him and tell him my plans. I'm certain he'll approve.

Finishing up our meal, we head back to the dorms. Oliver and I share a double with a private bathroom. We're moving off-campus next year, but as freshmen athletes, we were required to stay on campus this year. Neither one of us pledged a frat. We don't have time with school and baseball, and now I have Peyton. I always said I wouldn't have time for a girlfriend either, yet I'm making it a point to make time for her. I didn't know I'd meet someone who was perfect for me or that I would be eating those words, but I'm willing to admit I was wrong. It's tough, but we're going to make it happen.

As soon as we're in the dorm, I kick off my shoes and retrieve my laptop from my bag. I settle on my bed with my back against the wall, place my pillow on my lap, and video call Peyton.

"That was fast," she greets me with a smile.

"We were hungry and ready to get out of there. Two girls were hitting on us."

"Really? Did you get her number?"

"Nope. I pissed her off when I told her I was taken." I relay what happened, and she laughs.

"You could have taken it easy on her."

"Why would I? I don't want her or anyone who is not you touching me, even if it is just on the shoulder. And she didn't believe I was taken, and that pissed me off."

"You said you've not been much on commitment. Your reputation precedes you, Griff." Her smile is infectious.

"Let me see."

"I'm fine," she says, rolling her eyes.

"Let me see."

She winces as she moves her arm to the camera. "See, it's just a bruise."

"Damn, Peyton," Oliver says, leaning over the screen to take a look.

"Guys, it's fine."

"She's lying!" I hear Karina call out. "She's been whining since we got home today."

"I'm sorry I'm not there," I tell her.

This makes her laugh, but her eyes are soft. "Griffin, even if you were here, there is nothing you could do. This is all a part of the game. Our third string pitcher was on the mound, and I didn't move out of the way fast enough."

"Did you take anything?"

"Ice."

"Karina, get her some ibuprofen," I say loud enough, hoping she'll hear me.

"Already on it," she says, appearing on the screen. She hands Peyton pills and a glass of water.

"Hey, guys." Karina waves. "You keeping that one in line, Griff?" she asks, pointing at Oliver.

"He's been on his best behavior."

"I bet he has."

"No, really." I go on to tell her about the girls who were hitting on us earlier and how neither one of us took the bait. From the sound of it, Oliver is interested in her, and if I can be his wingman, then I will. Besides, we both blew them off. Sure, it was mostly me, but I have a feeling Oliver wouldn't have gone out with them anyway.

"What are you ladies getting into tonight?" Oliver asks.

"Staying in, watching a movie maybe."

"What are we watching?" I ask them.

Peyton laughs. "You watching with us again?"

"Yes." I leave no room for hesitation or negotiation in my answer. It's the next best thing to being there with her.

"I have some homework I need to wrap up."

"Me too. Should we start now?"

"Yeah, hold on. Let me grab my stuff." She hands her laptop to Karina.

"What about you? Are you going to study with us this time?" I ask her.

"Might as well." She shrugs.

I turn to look at Ollie. "You in?"

"Sure." He pretends not to be excited, but I know that look in his eyes. More time with Karina has them lighting up like the Fourth of July.

"Grab your laptop. I'll add you two to the call." He moves off my bed and to his and grabs his laptop. He gives me a thumbs-up when he's ready, and I add both him and Karina to the call. Grabbing my phone, I send him a text message.

Now you have her info.

Oliver:

I had her number.

But not her Zoom info.
Take notes, my man.

He replies with a thumbs-up. Tossing my phone to the side, I grab my books, and we get to work. We chat off and on while we each study. Karina asks for assistance with a calculus problem that Oliver graciously helps her with. The dude's a math whiz.

Two hours later, we've all had as much homework as we can stand. They order pizza, and so do we, and then we pull up Netflix and let the girls choose a movie. Thankfully, we have a flat-screen hanging on the wall, so we can all four stay connected to the call. It's cramped in this dorm room, but it works for us.

Peyton took me on a virtual tour of their apartment, and it looks like a mansion compared to our little space.

"How did you ladies luck out and get to live off-campus?" Oliver asks them as we're waiting for our pizza to be delivered. "I thought all athletes had to live on campus?"

"Well, I'm sure each school is different, but since we're local and technically not commuting, there's a certain mileage in there. They let us live at home. They just don't know we're staying in an apartment instead," Peyton explains.

"Griff, my man, why didn't we think about that?"

"I don't know, but I'm jealous as hell."

"I can't take the credit. Paisley figured it out when she went to college. Then Parker followed in her footsteps, and now me. It's the same college both of our parents went to as well, just not at the same time. Mom didn't go until after she had Paisley," she explains.

"Your sister is a genius," Oliver states.

"I'll be sure to tell her you said so."

The pizza arrives, and we settle into watching the movie. It's almost as if we're all in the same room together. We comment and laugh and joke, and the only thing that would make it better would be having her in my arms.

Once the movie is over, we all log off, and I switch to my phone, calling her and having some us time. We talk about school and living off-campus, and sports, and when we might be able to see each other again. Her voice is the last I hear before falling asleep, and I know it will also be the first when she calls me before she leaves for class in the morning.

Long distance? We've got this.

CHAPTER 13
Peyton

FOUR WEEKS. THAT'S HOW LONG it's been since I've been able to hug him—four very long weeks. I'm feeling it hard today and missing him like crazy. I only had one class this morning, and by some miracle, we don't have a game or practice today. Coach had something going on, so we got a pass.

Karina and a few of the girls on the team went shopping, and I chose to come home. I just wasn't feeling it. I wanted to be able to lie in bed and think about Griffin and wallow in my misery of missing him. I'll go back to a fully functioning individual tomorrow. Today, I just want to chill and watch mindless television, maybe read a book.

In fact, I'm in the middle of doing both when my cell rings. I have a movie playing in the background and my Kindle in my hand. Grabbing my phone, I smile when I see it's him. "Hey," I greet him. "I thought you would be at practice?"

"Coach let us out early. Are you getting ready to start? I just wanted to hear your voice."

"No, actually, I'm off today too. Coach had something come up, so no practice today."

"Really?" he asks. "So we don't have to hang up?"

"Nope. I'm lying in bed. I've got the TV on, and I was trying to read."

"Multitasking?" he guesses.

"More like trying to distract myself from missing you. It's been four weeks today since I've seen you."

"Yeah, I'm feeling it too. That's why I called, hoping to just hear your voice before you went to practice."

"This is hard."

"Yeah," he agrees.

"Are you having second thoughts?" I don't know why I ask the question when I already know the answer. Griffin is committed to making this relationship work, but sometimes, on days like today when I'm missing him like crazy, I second-guess that. I guess I just need to hear him say it.

"What? About us? No. No way. Are you?"

"No. I'm just really feeling it today. Missing you."

"Pretend I was there," he tells me. "What would we be doing?"

"Well, since we were both free from practice, games, and classes, my guess is you'd be lying next to me."

He groans. "Have I ever told you that I lie awake at night thinking about you lying next to me, skin to skin?"

"No," I whisper. "You've never told me."

"It happens a lot. I mean, I'm always thinking about you. You never leave my mind, but at night when it's quiet, and just me and my thoughts, I can almost feel you here in my arms."

"What are we doing? I mean, when I'm in your arms."

"I'm holding you."

"Is that all?" I ask. My voice is soft, and I can feel the heat in my cheeks at my question. I'm glad he can't see me.

"No, baby. That's not all."

"Tell me," I state boldly.

"Where's Karina?" he asks.

"Out with some of the girls from the team."

"You didn't want to go?"

"No. I wanted to come home and think about you. Where's Oliver?"

"He went to the beach with Sam and Daniel."

"You didn't want to go?"

"I told them I might meet them later. I wanted to come home and call you."

"You could have called me from the beach to say hello. You weren't even sure you would get ahold of me."

"Yeah, well, sometimes a guy just needs some time away from his roommate to do stuff."

"He's your best friend. What kind of stuff?" I ask.

"Guy stuff."

"Griffin."

"Fine." He sighs. "I'm missing the hell out of you, Peyton, and sometimes, well, a lot of times, I pull up the memory of you, of us, and take matters into my own hands."

"Tell me."

He groans. "It doesn't take much. Remembering the softness of your skin or the feel of your tongue stroking against mine."

"Are you... doing it now?" I swallow hard, and I'm sure he can hear me. It's more of a gulp as I process what's happening here.

"No."

"But you want to?"

"Yes."

"Are you hard for me?" I slap my hand over my mouth. I can't believe I just asked him that.

"God, yes," he moans.

"Hang up. I'm going to call you right back."

"What?" he chokes out. It's obvious that he's confused, but my brain is too jumbled to explain it to him.

"I promise. I'll call you right back." My voice doesn't sound like my own.

"Okay." The line goes dead, and I jump out of bed, grab my laptop from my desk, and lock my bedroom door for good measure. I pull up the video call and hit send. My hands are shaking, and my breathing kicks up a notch or three as I realize what I'm about to do. This is so unlike me. But maybe this is me with Griffin. What I feel for him, the way I miss him, and that trust that I have in him allows me to be free. Apparently, being free is phone sex or video-chat sex. Hell, I'm not sure what to call it, but it's about to go down.

"Hey," he greets huskily.

"Show me," I blurt out before I lose my nerve.

"What?" He chokes out a laugh.

"Please?" Maybe being demanding doesn't turn him on?

"Baby," he breathes. "You know I can't say no to you."

"Good." I smile. That's exactly what I was hoping for.

"But if I show you, you have to show me too." He gives me a pointed look, and I realize I didn't think this through. I just wanted to see him.

"I... uh..." I stumble over my words, and he chuckles.

"Do you touch yourself, Peyton? When you think of me?"

All the time. "Sometimes." There is no use in denying it. I can tell from the look in his eyes that he can see right through me.

"Show me." His voice is gravelly.

"I thought I was running this show?" I ask, my face flushed.

"Nah, we're in this together, remember?"

"That's what we said." The words are flippant, but the way my heart thunders in my chest at his sweet reminder isn't. *We're in this together.*

"Peyton?"

"Yeah?"

"Get naked."

"I..." I start to talk my way out of it but realize I don't want to. If I can't be with him, this is the next best thing. "Okay." Moving my laptop to the side, I climb out of bed. I'd already changed into a pair of sleep shorts and a T-shirt knowing that I was in for the day.

"I want to watch you," his gruff voice demands. "Turn the camera so I can see you."

Doing as he asks, I turn my laptop to face me. He can't see all of me, but when I remove my shirt and unclasp my bra, he sucks in a breath.

"Fuck, you're gorgeous."

"Griff?" My voice trembles, but it's not from nerves; it's more the excitement of what we're about to do.

"Yeah, baby?"

"Get naked." His boisterous laughter fills the room as I slide my shorts and panties over my thighs and down my legs. "And let me see you."

"So bossy," he quips.

"We're in this together." I toss his words back at him. My confidence grows with each second that passes. He wants this as much as I do.

He turns his screen so I can see. His T-shirt is the first to go, and his six-pack abs appear on the screen. His shorts hang loose on his hips, and the *V* that women go crazy for makes an appearance. His shorts go next, and I watch in fascination as he grips his cock and strokes it. He's rougher than I would have been, and I make a mental note for the next time we're together.

"Peyton." His voice is strained. "Touch yourself."

"Where?" Again, my voice doesn't sound like my own. It's all breathy and sensual, and so not like me.

He moans. "Your tits. Pretend it's me."

"Is that what you're doing? Pretending it's my hand that's stroking your cock?" Who am I? I've never talked like this in my life.

"Fuck yes," he says, his hand moving a little faster. "Pinch your nipples." I do as he says. "Damn," he mumbles.

"I don't know how to do this." The confession rolls off my tongue easily. This is *my* Griffin, so I can be honest with him.

"This is a first for me too. We just do what feels right?"

"Yeah," I agree, tweaking my nipple.

"Do you have a vibrator?"

"Y-Yes."

"Use it… or your fingers. I don't care. Just touch yourself. I need to see you."

Reaching into the nightstand, I pull out my hot-pink vibrator and climb on the bed. Instead of using it right away, I let my hands travel south, and when I reach the apex of my thighs, I stroke my clit.

"Have you used it? Since we got together?"

"Yes."

"Do you think about me?" he asks, his voice thick.

"Yes."

"Move the camera," he tells me. "I want to watch you."

I adjust my computer, and he sucks in a breath. "Fuck, I could come just like this. Just watching you."

"I want to see you."

He adjusts his screen as well, and my breath hitches when I see that he's now lying on the bed, and his hard length is wrapped up in his tight fist. He's not stroking himself, just holding his cock.

"Does it hurt?"

"To be away from you? Yes."

"No, I mean... your grip is so tight."

"I'm trying not to come."

"But isn't that the point?"

"You first, beautiful. You're always first."

"Together," I suggest.

"Grab your vibrator. Show me how you make yourself come."

"It doesn't take much when I think about you."

"Good. I'm losing my fucking mind over here."

Grabbing my battery-operated friend, I turn it on and hold it against my clit. I know this isn't exactly how I'm supposed to use it, but the vibration against my clit lets me know it's still doing its job. My back arches off the bed, and he hisses. My spare hand moves farther south, and I dip my finger inside.

"Jesus, I can hear how wet you are," he says, his voice strained.

"For you, Griffin." I close my eyes and just feel.

"Only for me."

"Yes," I say as my legs come together.

"No. No, open them. I need to watch you. Please." His voice is pleading.

Forcing myself to let my legs fall open, I also make my eyes do the same, and what I see on the screen pushes me over the edge. Just like that. All it takes is watching his hand gripping and stroking his cock. His grip is tight and his strokes are feverish as his hand strokes from root to tip. Seeing him pushes me over the edge of bliss as I fly apart at the seams. My orgasm rolls through me like a violent storm.

"Fuck, baby," Griffin grunts as he explodes all over his chest.

I watch with rapt attention as he comes down from the high of his release. "I wish I was there," I whisper. I would give anything to be next to him. To feel the heat of his skin pressed to mine.

"Me too, baby. Me too."

"I miss you."

"I miss you too."

"We should do… this more often," I suggest with a lazy, satisfied smile.

"I agree with you," he says. "I can't wait to see you in the flesh. I can't wait to hold you in my arms and feel you when you come."

"And now you have me ready to do it all over again," I tell him, and his laughter fills the room.

"Go get cleaned up, and I'll do the same. Call me when you're done. We'll watch a movie."

"Okay." Sliding off the bed, I go to end the call, but he's still connected. "Griff?"

"Yeah?"

"Thank you."

"Never thank me for being there for you or for pleasing you. It's just as much for me as it is for you."

"You're the best part of my day."

"You're the best part of my world. Go get cleaned up," he says.

I nod and end the call. My heart feels light and full at the same time. His words play a part in that, but so does he. Griffin, all on his own, gives me the reassurance and the determination that we're going to make this work.

I'm eager to get cleaned up and dressed so we can watch a movie together. When Griffin first suggested we try long-distance, I was sure it wouldn't work, but with each passing day, I might miss him terribly, but I feel closer to him. My doubts are gone, and in their place are memories of days like this one. We can do this.

CHAPTER 14
Griffin

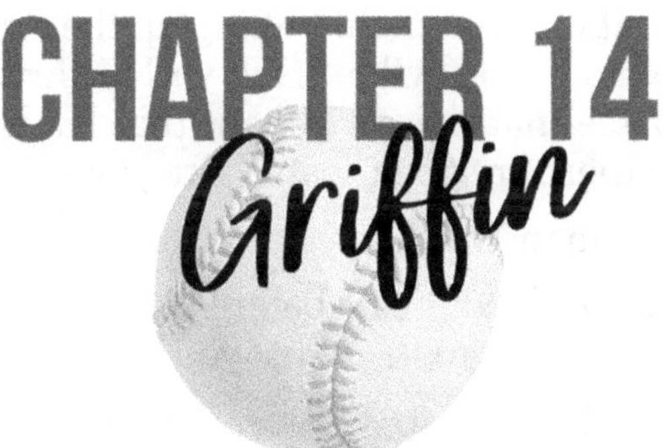

"THERE WAS A MIX-UP on the game schedule. This weekend's game is Friday, not Saturday," Coach says. We've just ended another grueling practice, but suddenly, I'm perked up.

Instantly an idea hits, and I can't help but be fucking excited about it. Coach finishes his speech, and we head to the locker room to get showered and changed. I'm smiling the entire time as the plan begins to form in my head.

"What's up with that?" Oliver points at my face.

"With what?" I play dumb. I know damn good and well what he's talking about.

"The cheesy smile. What gives?"

"We have two days off without a game."

"I heard Coach."

"Saturday is Peyton's birthday. I'm going to see her."

"No shit?" he asks. He's smiling too.

"And you're coming with me. This is your chance to talk to Karina."

"I doubt we can catch a flight this late."

"I'm about to find out." Shoving my stuff into my bag, I grab my phone and sit on the bench. Pulling up the airline's website, I check the flights to Nashville. "Hell yes!" I thrust my fist into the air when I see that there's a flight that lands at one in the afternoon, and there are open seats. "Are you in?" I ask him.

"Damn right I'm in."

That's all I need to hear before I book two tickets to Tennessee. "She's going to flip when you tell her."

"Yeah, I'm not going to tell her," I tell him, hitting the purchase button. My smile widens when it pops up that my order is complete.

"We don't know where they live, plus it's her birthday. What if she has plans?"

"She does. She already told me her mom is making her favorite dinner."

"You're just going to crash it?"

"Yep. It's been five fucking weeks since I've seen her outside of a damn computer screen. Hell yes, I'm crashing."

"You're going to need backup."

"I know. I'm going to text Karina now."

Hey, is Peyton around you?

Karina:

No, I'm at the library.

Good. Can you step out so I can call you?

Karina:

Griffin Anthony, if you're
about to break her heart,
I'm hopping on the next
flight to Florida and
kicking your ass.

Never. I told you that.

Karina:

Fine. I'll call you when
I'm outside. I was
getting ready to leave
anyway, so I needed to
pack up my stuff.

Thank you.

"She's at the library. She's going to call me once she gets outside."

"Is Peyton with her?"

"No. It's like this was meant to be."

"You're meeting the parents," he reminds me.

I shrug. "She's already met mine. It's only fair that I meet hers. Besides, they need to get used to me being in her life. I'm not going anywhere."

"If I didn't know better, I'd say you're pussy-whipped," he teases.

I laugh. "It's more like Peyton-whipped. She's got me under her spell," I say just as my phone rings. Grabbing my bag and tossing it over my shoulder, I show Oliver the screen. "I'll meet you at the Jeep," I tell him and swipe the screen. "Hello."

"What's up?"

"Our schedule was printed wrong. Our game is Friday instead of Saturday."

"Okay."

"I just bought a flight to Nashville for Saturday." It takes maybe three seconds for her brain to register what I just said.

"Holy shit! She's going to flip."

"I hope so." I laugh. "Anyway, I want to surprise her. I don't know where you live or where her parents live. I know she's having dinner there on Saturday."

"What time does your flight land?"

"One."

"Okay. We have to be at her parents' place at five. Let me call her sisters, and I'll get back to you."

"You can give me their numbers if you want, and I'll call them."

"Maybe, but I don't like to do that. Especially with Paisley and Parker, considering who they are married and soon-to-be engaged to."

"Fair enough. Let me know."

"I'm on it. I'll call or text you soon."

"Thanks, Karina. Oh, and just so you know, Ollie is coming with me."

"Is he?" she asks. I can hear the interest and maybe even a little excitement in her voice.

"He's one of the good ones," I tell her.

"I'll keep that in mind," she replies. "We'll talk soon."

"I heard that," Oliver says from behind me.

"I wasn't trying to hide it. I was being a good wingman."

He shakes his head, but there's a smile pulling at his lips. "Come on, Romeo, I'm starving."

Tossing our bags in the back of my Jeep, we head to my parents' place. I need to tell them I'm leaving town this weekend, and I know there's always something mouthwatering waiting for me in their fridge. We might have to hang around until they get home, but that's fine too. Now that I don't live at home, I can't keep up with their schedules, mine, and Peyton's.

☙❍❧

"So Parker's picking us up?" Oliver asks as we deboard the plane.

"Yes. I told her we could get a rental, but she insisted. I wasn't going to argue with her."

"And we're staying with the girls?"

"Yeah. Karina knows that Peyton's going to want me to stay with her, and she said the two of you could catch up."

"Nice." He grins.

Since we're only here for one night, we have one carry-on each. Making our way through the airport, I see Parker and recognize Paisley from the pictures Peyton has shown me as the woman standing next to her, and that must mean that the little boy in the stroller is Jett, her nephew.

"Griffin!" Parker smiles and rushes forward, hugging me. "She's going to be blown away when she finds out that you're here."

"I hope so. I hate that it's only for one night, but I'll take what I can get." I turn to Oliver. "This is my best friend, Oliver. Ollie, this is Parker, Peyton's middle sister, and I'm guessing this is Paisley, her older sister."

"He's good." Paisley beams.

"Told you," Parker boasts.

I crouch down and offer my fist to Jett. Peyton told me he loves to fist bump. He doesn't hesitate to bump knuckles. "You must be Jett. My name is Griffin. It's nice to meet you."

"You's Pey's friend," he announces.

"That's right. I am. I'm here to surprise her."

He nods and goes back to munching on the small container of Goldfish crackers in his lap. I stand back to my full height. "Thank you for coming to get us. We could have rented a car."

"No way," Paisley replies. "This is going to be epic. She's been mopey all week, and you are going to cheer her up. I can't wait until she sees you."

"So what's the plan?"

"Well, we thought it would be best if you're at Mom and Dad's when she gets there."

"Okay. What time is she coming?"

"Mom told her we're eating at five, so she'll be there a little before that."

"And until then?" I ask.

"You get to hang out with the family. It will give us a chance to get to know you better."

"By family, you mean your parents?" Oliver asks.

"Yep." Paisley grins.

"Is that okay?" Parker asks.

"Yeah. I just know how your dad reacted to Cameron and Holden, and they have a hell of a lot more going for them than I do. They were already in the league, and I'm just a college player with aspirations."

"That's not true," Parker tells me. "Peyton told us all about your double major. That's a lot for a student-athlete. And you can't take our dad too seriously. He didn't like Cameron and Holden, not because of the men they were, but because they were dating us. He's protective like that. Sometimes, I wish we had a brother he could have bonded with, but then I think about how Dad would have brainwashed him to be just as protective, and I'm glad it's just us girls." She laughs.

"I'm in regardless," I tell them.

"We'll keep Dad in check, and we've brought Mom on board. They know you're coming, and she's going to keep him reeled in."

"Okay. Well, let's do this." Oliver and I follow them out of the airport and into the parking garage. Paisley drove her SUV. We toss our bags in the back and then slide in on either side of Jett's car seat. He jabbers on about his daddy and baseball and his pappa, which I'm guessing is how he refers to Peyton's dad. The trip is quick, and before I know it, we're pulling into a huge-ass house with a gated driveway that's long and paved.

"Are you ready for this?" Oliver asks.

"Yes."

Parker turns in her seat to look at me. "Awfully confident," she teases. There's a glint of happiness in her eyes, and it reminds me of Peyton.

"It's inevitable. I'm not willing to give her up, so this is just the progression of our relationship. Besides, she met my parents."

"Yeah, but you were there with her," Oliver counters.

"In about three hours, I get to see my girlfriend, who I haven't had my arms around in five long weeks. There isn't anything I wouldn't endure to make that happen."

"Damn," Paisley mutters.

"Mommy. Dat's a bad word," Jett tells her.

"Mommy's sorry," she tells him. "But Uncle Griffin just made Mommy swoon."

Jett turns to look at me. "You's my uncle?" he asks, his little brows furrowed.

"Not yet, little man, but one day," I tell him. It's a big claim to make in front of her sisters and her nephew, but it's where I want this to go.

"See what I've been living with?" Oliver jokes.

"I think it's sweet," Parker tells me.

"I'm just being me." I shrug.

"Well, we better get in there. I'm sure Mom's excited to meet you, and Dad, well, he's going to be cold, but just be you." Paisley meets my eyes in the rearview mirror. "He needs to see the real you. Don't hold back from him, and don't let him intimidate you.

He's going to need to see that you're here for her and nothing else."

"Trust me. That's why I'm here." I don't plan to hold back. It's not possible even if I really tried, not after five long weeks without her. He needs to get used to me being around. I plan to visit as much as my schedule allows.

"I believe you, but we've," she motions between her and Parker, "learned a few things with introducing Dad to Cam and Holden. We're passing that wisdom on to you."

"I appreciate it, but I'm fine."

"Yeah," Paisley agrees. "I think you're going to be just fine."

"I'll grab Jett," Parker says. "Cam will flip out if he finds out I let you carry him."

"I'm fine. I'm pregnant, not injured."

"I'll get him."

"I want Uncle Griff," Jett tells them.

"Well, all right then." Parker laughs. "Just leave your bags in the back. Unless you need something from them?"

"I'm good," Oliver and I say at the same time.

"Let's do this." Parker and Paisley climb out of the SUV.

I fumble with the straps of the car seat, but I'm able to release them and lift Jett into my arms. "You's big like Daddy," he says.

"He is tall like Daddy." Paisley smiles at her son.

"I want Daddy," Jett says. It's not a cry, more like a statement.

"He's working. They're surprisingly off today, but they had practice. He and Uncle Holden will be here later."

"I hab lots of uncles."

"You have two uncles," Parker says, winking at me.

My chest swells for this little boy and this family who have been so accepting. Well, so far. I have yet to meet her parents, and I'm nervous because I want them to like me.

"We're here!" Parker calls out.

"Come with us," Paisley tells us.

With Jett still perched on my hip, I follow them down the hall and into the living room. I can feel Oliver standing beside me in silent support. This is a big deal for me. I'm meeting my girl's parents, but it's also a big deal as a baseball fan for Oliver and me. We were both huge fans of Easton's growing up, so this is surreal for us in that aspect as well.

"Mom, Dad, this is Griffin and his best friend, Oliver. Griffin, this is our mom, Larissa, and our dad, Easton."

"It's a pleasure to meet you both." I offer Larissa my hand first, and she waves it off, hugging Jett and me at the same time, making him laugh. She steps back, and I offer my hand to Easton. He stares at it until his wife elbows him in the ribs, and he finally reaches out and shakes my hand.

"Come to Pappa." He holds his arms out for Jett.

"Uncle Griff gots me," Jett tells him, and I can practically see the steam coming from Easton's ears.

"He's not your uncle."

"Mommy said so," he tells Easton.

"That's right. I did," Paisley tells him. "Pappa just forgot what Griffin means to Aunt Peyton."

"And he made Mommy swoon," Jett adds helpfully.

I make a mental note that this kid doesn't miss anything.

"Be nice," Larissa tells her husband.

"He's stealing my grandson," Easton counters. "And my lady," he mumbles, but we all hear him.

"Come on, Dad." Paisley rolls her eyes. "No one is stealing anything."

"Fine. We'll lay it out then. He's a college ballplayer. He found out that your sister was connected to the game in more ways than one, and now he's using her to get to us and to get to the league."

"Hey, Jett. Why don't you go to your aunt Parker?" I hand him to Parker. "Can you take him out of the room for a minute?" I ask her.

She looks at Paisley. "Record this," she mouths, and Paisley grins but pulls her cell out of her pocket. If I weren't so pissed off right now, I'd laugh at their antics.

I wait for Parker to leave the room before I open my mouth and let my emotions take over. "I didn't know who she was, at least not the way you're insinuating. To me, she was a beautiful woman with a smile that lit up the already bright sky. I wanted to spend more time with her before I found out her last name and your family's connection to the game I love. Yes, I love baseball. I've played since I was Jett's age, and I'm damn good at it. I'd love to be one of the lucky ones to make it to the league, but I know that's a long shot, and I'm planning for that not to happen, just as much as I'm planning and wishing that it would. That's my dream, and it has nothing to do with your daughter. That's a new dream and one that came to be after I met her. I know regardless of my future with the game that I love, that I'll be able to provide for her and the family that we will hopefully one day have."

"You just met her," he counters, crossing his arms over his chest.

I shrug. "You met your wife and fell for her instantly. What makes you think that I can't do that as well?"

"How do you know that?"

"Peyton. We talk about everything. I feel like I know her better than I know myself."

"Then you know she wouldn't appreciate you talking to me like this in my home."

"Actually, sir, I'd like to think that she'd be proud of me. You see, your daughter also knows that growing up, I was a huge fan of yours. Oliver too." I nod to my friend, who has a smirk pulling at his lips. "She knows that about me, but do you know what else she knows?"

"Enlighten me." Easton crosses his arms over his chest.

"She knows that she comes first for me. I'd walk away from all of it today if it meant I could be with her."

"Then why don't you?" he fires back.

"She won't let me," I tell him honestly.

"You could do it anyway."

"I could," I agree. "But I have a full ride where I am, and I've already got league scouts coming to see my games. I'm fifteen minutes from my family, and if my dreams of one day going pro come true, I'll more than likely be moving away from them. Peyton told me to stay... that it's better to be close to them while I can."

"That sounds like her," Larissa speaks up. "She's always been wise beyond her years."

"Daddy!" Jett's cheers filter into the room.

"You've already met my husband and future brother-in-law," Paisley says, smiling at her dad, and he grumbles under his breath. "Why don't we go say hi."

I nod, but I'm not finished yet. "I care about your daughter. I more than care about her, but I think she needs to hear those words from me before you do." With that, I turn and follow Paisley and Oliver out of the room.

Parker holds her hand out, and Paisley hands over her phone. The group gathers around, watching the scene that just went down in the living room.

"My man." Holden holds his hand out for me to shake, followed by Cameron.

"We calmed him down for you," Cameron jokes.

"Right? You got off easy," Holden agrees.

We all chat for a few minutes before we settle once again in the living room and wait for Peyton to arrive.

"I think we should lock the door, and you should answer it." Parker claps her hands with glee.

"I'll gladly be the first person she sees," I tell them. They all laugh as Parker scurries to lock the front door.

CHAPTER 15
Peyton

IT'S BEEN FIVE WEEKS SINCE I've seen Griffin in person and not through a computer screen. We talk multiple times a day, and each night we video call before we switch over to the phone to say good night. We send multiple text messages throughout our days, and I feel closer to him than anyone. I wasn't sure we could do this, but we're making it happen. It's hard, and I miss him, but we're making it work.

However, today it's hitting me hard. Today is my birthday. It's just another day, but that doesn't stop me from wishing he was here with me today. It's Saturday, and my mom insisted on having dinner and inviting everyone. I appreciate the effort, but the one person I want to see won't be there.

"You about ready to head out?" Karina asks.

"I'm ready when you are," I say, standing from the couch.

"Is that what you're wearing?" she asks.

I look down at my Capri leggings and Blaze T-shirt. "What's wrong with what I'm wearing?"

"Peyton, come on. Your mom is planning this for you, and your entire family will be there. At least make it look like you care just a little." She places her hands on her hips and stares me down.

"They're my family. They don't care how I'm dressed."

"You're right. But you might not be so mopey if you spruce up a little. Come on. I'll help you." She places her hands on my shoulders and turns me down the hall toward my bedroom.

"Fine," I grumble as I plop down on my bed.

"Here." She hands me a pair of boyfriend jeans with rips in the knees. "Wear these and this." She hands me a gray flowing tank top and a blue-and-white-and-gray flannel. "You can roll your sleeves up or take it off if you get too hot."

I look at her, and she's dressed in a similar way. Her jeans are darker than mine, but she's also wearing a flowing tank and a three-quarter sleeve cardigan over it. "Fine." I stand and quickly change my outfit. "Shoes?" I might as well let her finish off the ensemble.

"Your dark gray Hey Dudes will be fine."

"At least you have good taste." I chuckle as I take the shoes and slide them onto my feet. "Now what?"

"Now, you let me put some curls in your hair and add just a soft touch of makeup."

"Really? Is that necessary?"

"Yes. Look, I know you're missing him, but when you call him later, he's going to be sad and missing you too. You know that man is crazy about you. If he thinks for a second that you're here moping, it's going to eat him alive. Do this for Griffin."

"You're right," I concede. I move to the bathroom and sit on the toilet, letting her curl my hair, and then add some light makeup. By the time she's done, I not only look better, but I feel better too. "Thank you, Karina."

"That's what best friends are for. Now, give me your phone. I want to take a picture of you to send to your man."

I smile wide, handing her my phone. She takes the picture and hands it back to me. "Send it now. Let's see what he says."

Doing as she says, I type out a message, followed by the picture.

> Missing you more today than yesterday.

Griffin:
> You take my breath away.

> This is hard, Griffin.

Griffin:
> I know. I miss you too.

> I gotta go. My mom is having dinner and invited my sisters and their families.

Griffin:
> Have fun, birthday girl. Call me later?

> You know I will.

I slide my phone into my purse and look up to find Karina watching me. "Well, what did he say?"

"That he misses me and that I take his breath away." My cheeks heat. It's not like she hasn't already heard him say that exact thing. She's here a lot when we video call, and she bend Oliver have joined us on our study sessions more often than not. Griffin doesn't hold back his feelings and doesn't care who hears him.

The other day, he was in the locker room after the home game they won when he called me. He was telling me he missed me and wished I was there. His teammates were razzing him, but he just laughed it off and told them they were just jealous. He didn't have a single care that they heard him telling me that he missed me.

"He's one of the good ones, Peyton."

"I think so too."

"But?"

"We've only spent a handful of days together."

"What about the past five weeks?"

"Gah! I know. This is so freaking hard. I second-guess everything, but when we're talking, the doubt disappears."

"Come on, birthday girl. Let's go hang with your family and eat our weight in cake and ice cream, so you can come home and call your man."

"How is it possible to fall this hard for someone you can't touch or kiss?" I ask her as we make our way out to her car.

"I think that this is better," she says, climbing behind the wheel.

"How so?" I ask once we're on the road.

"You're getting to know one another. There is no pressure for sex. You two are taking the time to talk about anything and everything. You know each other to your core. The other stuff, the sex, and kissing, and all that other stuff you're missing, it's just fluff."

"What if I want the fluff?"

She laughs. "Oh, honey, we all want the fluff. What I'm saying is that when you two reach that point, when you get there, you're already going to be so in tune with each other that it's bound to be magical. It's going to mean more. It's not going to be just an orgasm, but it's going to be more."

"I guess I never really thought about it like that."

"Trust me. Remember my first time?" she asks. "We were both inexperienced and had no idea what we were doing."

"And now?"

"Now, I like to think I know what I like, and I'm not afraid to ask for it. You shouldn't be either."

"I don't really know..." My voice trails off.

"You will. When it happens, you will, and you have to tell him. I'm kind of jealous, to be honest."

"What? Why would you be jealous?"

"Because if the way that he looks at you is any indication, he's going to listen to everything you tell him. He's going to make it happen and rock your world."

"Stop!" I laugh. "No worlds are being rocked. I don't know when I'll see him again."

"But when you do, it will be that much sweeter."

I don't reply to that, because what do I say? I have no idea if what she's saying is right, but I want it to be. With the little bit of time we had with each other, I know he lights my body on fire. The thought of telling him what I want, what feels good, has me blushing. I guess the only saving grace is that it will be a first for him too. We can fumble through it together.

When we pull into my parents' driveway, it's already full. "Sheesh, what time is it? Are we late or something? She said five, right?" I ask Karina.

"It's ten till," she tells me. "Maybe everyone is just excited to see you and eat cake." She shrugs.

"Maybe."

"Besides, you're close with your sisters. You don't want to see them?"

"It's not that. I want to see them and Jett, of course. And Paisley is ready to deliver their baby girl any day. I just wish things were different."

"Come on." She pulls the keys from the ignition. "None of that talk. When we get home tonight, you can video call him and tell him all about it."

"You're right," I agree and reach for the door handle to climb out of her car.

Karina links her arm through mine, and together, we walk up the sidewalk and to the front door. I go to open it, but it's locked. "What the heck? I wonder why the door is locked. I don't have my keys," I tell her. She drove, and I didn't think I'd need them. Irritated, since they knew I was coming, I ring the doorbell three times and knock for good measure.

"I think they heard you the first ring and was the knock necessary?" Karina laughs.

I turn to look at her. "Hush. They knew we were on our way. I mean, they're all here for my birthday." I sound like a spoiled brat, but I can't seem to find it in me to care.

The sound of the door lock moving has me turning my head. I stand impatiently as the door slowly opens. I blink once, twice, three times before hot tears race down my cheeks.

"Am I dreaming?" I turn to ask Karina.

"You're not dreaming."

"Peyton." Griffin breathes my name as he steps out onto the porch and wraps me in his arms. "Fuck, baby, I've missed you," he whispers just for me.

"How are you here right now?" I ask, pulling back to smile up at him through my tears.

He cradles my face in his hands and wipes at my tears with his thumbs. "I couldn't miss my girl's birthday."

"Your girl's father is standing right here," my dad says from the doorway.

"You came here to meet them without me?"

Griffin chuckles. "I did."

"Are you coming inside?" Dad asks.

I step away from Griffin and link his hand with mine. Turning to face the door, my parents are standing in front, and everyone else in my family is gathered behind them to watch the reunion.

"Oliver?" I ask.

He waves with a wide grin. "Hey, Peyton. Happy Birthday."

"Thank you." I chuckle, then turn my attention back to my parents. "I know you already met him, but Mom, Dad, this is Griffin." I turn to smile up at him. "My boyfriend."

"We've met," Dad says, and Mom elbows him.

"Come on in. Dinner is ready. I made your favorite," Mom says.

"Lasagna?"

"You know it." Stepping back, she pulls my dad with her, giving us room to come inside.

"Come on, Dad." Paisley laughs. "This is round three. You should be used to this by now," she teases.

"I'll never get used to seeing men maul my baby girls."

"It's been weeks since we've seen each other," I defend, refusing to let go of Griffin's hand.

"You're too young for..." Dad twirls his hand around, pointing at Griffin and me. "That," he finally says.

I thought I would be stressed out if and when Griffin met my family, but I'm so excited he's here that I don't even care that my dad is acting a fool. "Sorry, Daddy," I say sweetly. "He's sticking around."

"Figures," he grumbles. With Mom tugging on his arm, he follows her into the kitchen.

"You're welcome," Paisley and Parker say at the same time.

"What?" I ask, confused.

"We prepared him for this day. Cam and Holden got his wrath," Paisley reminds me.

"You're getting off easy," Cam tells Griffin.

"So you've said." He laughs. "I'm willing to take all of it." Griffin pulls me into his arms.

"Aw." Paisley smiles before turning to look at Parker. "You're right. He is the best."

"Hey," Cam says, kissing her cheek and placing his hand on her swollen belly.

"You're still the very best," she soothes her husband.

"And what about you?" Holden crosses his arms over his chest and frowns at Parker.

She leans up on her tiptoes and presses her lips to his. "You're my number one."

"Damn right," he says, pulling her close and kissing her as if no one else is standing in the room.

"Bailey!" Dad booms. "What did I tell you about that shit? Cut it out," Dad grumbles, making the room erupt in laughter.

"Come on, let's go eat." I turn to Karina. "Can you save Oliver?" I laugh.

"I'm on it." She moves to stand by Oliver, giving him a hug and leading him into the kitchen.

I don't move, and neither does Griffin, as my family filters out of the foyer. When it's just the two of us, I turn to face him. He bends at the knees, places his hands on the back of my thighs, and lifts me. I wrap myself around him and bury my face in his neck.

"I can't believe you're here."

"I had to see you on your birthday."

"How long do you get to stay?"

"We fly out tomorrow afternoon."

"So soon?" I ask, already feeling tears well in my eyes.

"I'm not leaving your side until I have to get on that plane," he assures me.

I lift my head to look into his eyes. I want him to see the sincerity of my words. "Thank you, Griff. I was missing you something fierce today, and I was in a pissy mood, and I just... I can't believe you're here."

He rests his forehead against mine. "I missed you, too, and I told you. We've got this."

"Lady?" I hear my dad's voice behind us.

Griffin slowly lowers me to my feet, and I turn to face my father. "We'll be right there."

My dad studies me for a few long seconds before nodding and leaving us alone.

"I love that he calls you lady. Earlier, he was talking about you to your sisters and using their names as well. I told him it was genius, and you were right. He kind of puffed his chest out a little," he tells me.

"Oh, so you were sucking up to him?" I tease.

"Hey. You're the one who told me I should tell him that I loved the names when I met him."

"Come on, let's go eat some of my mom's famous lasagna." Hand in hand, we make our way into the kitchen to make our plates. We're the last two to settle in the dining room. Griffin and I take the last two chairs that happen to be at the opposite end of the table as my parents.

Holden and Cam pull him into a conversation about his season. "You're kicking ass on the mound," Cam praises.

"It's been a good season," Griffin replies.

"You're a pitcher?" my dad asks.

"Yes, sir."

"Are you any good?"

"Dad," Parker scolds him. "You just heard Cam tell him he was kicking ass on the mound."

Dad shrugs. "Could be luck."

Griffin turns to look at me. "Yeah," he says wistfully. "I'm definitely having a lucky year."

I don't make eye contact with anyone but him. My heart is pounding in my chest, and all I want to do is kiss him. So that's what I do. I lean into him and press my lips to his cheek.

"Lady," Dad warns.

"Easton," Mom scolds him.

"I'm sorry, sir," Griffin speaks up.

"You don't have anything to apologize for. I kissed you, and it was just a peck on the cheek."

"Baby, he's your dad. One day, I'm going to need him to tell me I have his blessing to marry you, and I kinda need him to like me for that to happen."

My mouth drops open in shock, and from the silence of the room, I think everyone else is too. It's my mother who breaks the silence.

"I can't tell you how happy it makes me to see that each of my girls has found men who care about them." She turns to look at my dad. "All three of them remind me of you when we were dating. In fact, I can hear you saying something similar. Easton, look around you. Our daughters are happy and healthy, and the men in their lives are honest and respectful and treat them like the queens we've raised them to be."

"She's too young for talk about marriage."

"He didn't say today, Dad," I sass.

"She's an adult, and she has a good head on her shoulders. We have to trust that she's making the best choices for her," Mom counters. "Read the room, Easton. Look at how these three young men are looking at our daughters."

"I married mine," Cam chimes in.

"Show off," Holden grumbles, making us all laugh.

"Regardless, our daughters are happy and in healthy relationships. What more could we ask for?"

"For them to all still be living at home?" Dad offers.

"Stop." Mom leans over and kisses his cheek. "I love you, Easton Monroe."

"Stop." Parker covers her eyes. "We don't need to see all of that."

"Like it's not something we've seen every single day of our lives," Paisley adds.

"You taught us what it means to be loved the right way. You have to trust that we'll accept nothing less than what you and Mom have."

I watch my father as he swallows hard and nods. "You're right. The three of you are strong, independent women, and I trust that you know what's best for you." He makes a point to look at me and then each of my sisters. "However, for the three of you, and you—" Dad points at Oliver for good measure. "—they're my entire world. If you hurt them, you'll never get near them again."

"What, no death threats?" Cam jokes.

"Taylor," Dad warns.

"Dat's my name." Jett points at his chest. "Jett Taylor," he says proudly, and my dad visibly softens.

"Yeah, buddy," Dad agrees. "That's your name."

"And you know our kids' names are going to be Bailey, right?" Holden says, just to get under Dad's skin.

Cam and Holden both have a great relationship with my father, and he may act annoyed, but he secretly adores them.

"And you know, if this thing works out," I wave between Griffin and me—"mine will be Anthony."

Dad points at me, his lips lifting just slightly. "Too soon, lady. Too soon."

The table erupts with laughter, and we finish our meal. Everyone pulls both Griffin and Oliver into the conversation as if they've known them for years, and it turns out to be the best birthday yet.

CHAPTER 16
Griffin

I'D BE LYING IF I said I wasn't nervous about meeting her dad. From the stories she's told me, I knew he was protective. I've never met my girlfriend's parents before, so I didn't know what I was up against. I was grateful Oliver came with me and that Parker was the one to meet us. She was on our side. At least Peyton says that she is.

I was sweating bullets until my girl got here. It was her sister's idea to lock the door and have me answer it. Her dad didn't agree, but her mom was able to convince him. He's this protective bear when it comes to his family, but it's easy to see that Larissa, his queen, can talk him off the ledge.

Thankfully.

We had dinner, and we've all been sitting around talking. I'm sitting on the floor, leaning my back against the couch between Peyton's legs. Her dad keeps eyeing me, but I ignore it. I've been away from her for five long, agonizing weeks. I'm not leaving her side.

She leans forward, placing her hands on my shoulders. "You about ready to go?" she asks.

I turn to look at her. "Where are we going?"

"My place."

"Griffin." Her dad speaks up. I turn back around to give him my attention. "Where are you all staying?"

"With me," Peyton answers.

Easton Monroe's face is blood red. "Lady," he starts, but he's cut off when Larissa places her hand over his mouth.

"She's an adult, Easton."

"I don't like it," he grumbles.

"You don't have to like it, but you do have to deal with it." He grumbles under his breath but doesn't say another word.

I don't tell them that I didn't reserve a room. I was hoping that Peyton would be okay with us crashing with them, but if not, we could have just found a hotel to stay in. Karina assured me that she would be, and she was right.

"We're going to go," Peyton says, tapping my shoulder for me to stand. I climb to my feet and offer her my hand, helping her from the couch. Not that she needed the help, but it's another excuse to touch her without her father trying to shoot me. Okay, "shoot" might be a little over the top, but he's definitely not happy that I'm here.

"Thank you for dinner and the gifts," Peyton tells the room. She then hugs every person in the room until she ends up back beside me. She slides her arm around my waist and smiles up at me.

"Ready?" she asks.

I nod and step away from her and move toward her father. I hold my hand out for him to shake. "It was nice to meet you, sir."

Easton gives me a curt nod but shakes my hand. I offer my hand to Larissa with the same sentiment, but she pulls me into a hug. "You're welcome here anytime," she assures me.

I hug her sisters, shake hands with Cameron and Holden, and fist bump with Jett, and we're out the door.

"We're moving in," Oliver says as we step inside the girls' apartment. "This place is quadruple the size of our dorm room."

"Well, it's only a two-bedroom, so we're going to need to talk sleeping arrangements if the two of you move in." Karina laughs.

"That's easy. I'm rooming with Peyton," I tell her.

Oliver grins. "And you and I can share," he tells Karina.

"Just like that?" she asks.

"Yup." He doesn't even blink as he gauges her reaction.

She laughs. "Well, all right then. You get the couch tonight unless you promise to behave. I have a queen, so if you can stay on your side, you can sleep with me."

I watch as my best friend opens his mouth to speak, but no words come out. Instead, he nods and buries his hands in his pockets. We talked on the flight here, and he said he was going to tell her he liked her and wanted to test the waters. It looks like he's going to get his chance.

"How about a movie?" Karina suggests.

I look over at Peyton, and I can see she wants to say no, but she nods her agreement. That's fine with me. I'm here with her, and that's what matters. Kicking off my shoes, I drop my bag behind the couch. I move to where she's standing and take her hand in mine. Together, we move to the couch. I sit and pull her onto my lap.

"On second thought, maybe the two of you should call it a night." Oliver laughs.

"You don't have to tell me twice." I stand with her in my arms. "Which room is yours, babe?"

"First door on the left."

"Enjoy the movie," I tell our friends as I carry her down the hall and push open her bedroom door. I drop her on the bed with a bounce, making her laugh. "You're wearing too many clothes," I tell her.

"Oh, really? What do you think I should do about that?"

"Strip."

"What about you?" she asks.

Reaching for the hem of my shirt, I pull it over my head. "You got some catching up to do." Dropping my shirt on the floor, I reach for the button on my jeans and lower it before sliding my jeans and underwear to the floor, kicking them to land on my shirt.

"Baby, it's been five weeks since I've felt your skin next to mine. Please, for the love of everything holy, get naked." I grip my cock, and gently stroke as I watch her begin to undress.

Once she's completely naked, she slides under the covers, pulling them up to her chin. "Is there room under there for me?" I ask her.

"You're the only one I'd make room for."

My palms are sweating. It's not that I'm nervous. It's more excitement to hold her. Moving to the door, I turn the lock and hit the overhead light before climbing under the covers next to her. The room is lit with a soft glow from the bedside lamp. She immediately moves closer and curls her body around mine. "Damn," I murmur.

"I missed you. I missed this," she whispers.

Instead of telling her that I missed her, I show her. I switch our positions where she's lying flat on her back, and I'm hovering over her. She opens her legs, and I settle between her thighs. My cock is nestled against her pussy, and I can feel how wet she is. It wouldn't take much for me to slip inside and feel her. Instead, I kiss her. I stroke Peyton's lips with my tongue, and she immediately opens for me.

Her legs lock around my waist, and she buries her hands in my hair. I swivel my hips, and she moans. The sound goes straight to my cock, which twitches, and this time it's me who's moaning.

I'm close. I can feel my spine start to stiffen, and I can't let that happen. I can't get off just from kissing her. I mean, I can, but I don't want to. She needs to go first.

"Griff?"

"Peyton?"

"Can we... try something?"

"What do you want to try?"

"Lie back on the bed." Curious as hell, I give her one more kiss before moving to lie flat on the bed. I'd never deny her anything.

"Now what?" She bites down on her bottom lip. Lifting my hand, I pull her lip free with my thumb. "Whatever it is, I'm in."

She smiles as her cheeks flush. "You don't know that."

"I do know that. I can't say no to you. I don't want to say no to you. You can tell me anything, and if it's within my power, I'm going to make it happen."

"Gah!" She covers her face with her hands. "Why am I so nervous?"

I don't think the question is for me, but I answer her anyway. "You don't have to be. It's just me, Peyton. I'm all yours, remember?"

"I thought we could try it at the same time?"

"Try what?"

"I could do what I did before, and you could too, but we could, you know..." She shrugs. "Do it together. At the same time."

Oh, fuck. "Babe, we can do that, but I need to tell you that I'm probably not going to last."

Her smile is shy. "That's the point, Griff."

"No, what I'm telling you is I was already close to coming from just kissing you and having your skin against mine. If my face is buried in your pussy while you suck my cock, I'm going to go off like a rocket."

"Griffin." She's smiling, but her face is beet red. "We don't have to," she says quickly.

"Oh, no. It's happening. I just wanted to add a disclaimer that I'll probably get off first, and I want it to be you."

"Does it really matter as long as we both get there?"

"It matters to me. You always go first."

"Well, today is my birthday, and I miss you, and I want to try it, and I want to try it with you."

"Damn right with me. Only me."

"Only you."

"Peyton?"

"Yeah?" she says, staring down at her hands.

"Look at me." She lifts her head, and I motion for her to come closer. She does as I ask, and I slide my hand behind her neck and kiss her soundly. Pulling back, I look her in the eyes and say, "Time to sit on my face."

She cracks up laughing, and I swat her ass. "Hey."

"This is your fantasy. I'm just the executer."

"We don't have to." She tries to get out of it.

"Nope. Turn around and back that ass up." I wink.

I watch as she turns and straddles me, her back to my front. "I don't know how to do this. I don't know what I was thinking."

"Hey." I run my hand down her back. "It's just me. I don't care what it is you want to try. I'm your partner in this, right? In life? You can always be open with me about what you want."

She peers at me over her shoulder. "Griff, I…" She takes a deep breath. "Okay. Here goes nothing." She moves her ass farther up my chest and lies down, her face hovering over my cock.

Gripping her hips, I slide lower on the bed and position her legs on either side of my face. My mouth waters at the sight of her. I'm glad I left the lamp on. I definitely would have been disappointed to miss this. When I feel her hand grip my cock, I lean forward and taste her.

Her tongue licks my cock like a lollipop, and part of me wishes I could watch the show, but the one I have in front of me is good too. Gripping her ass cheeks, I get to work. I bury my face in her pussy, and she squirms when my tongue covers her clit, but I hold her still. I show her with my mouth, with my tongue, and yes, even my teeth how much I've missed her over the past five weeks.

My cock falls from her mouth, and she moans my name, making me smile. I ease up just a little, and she gets back to work, taking me to the back of her throat. This time it's me who's coming up for air and moaning her name.

"Fuck, Peyton." I pull in a deep breath, trying to prolong this, but there's no use. I'm not coming without her, so I go back in, and it only takes a few more seconds before I taste her release on my tongue. Her body shakes, and she moans around my cock, and I release into her hot mouth.

Somehow, we manage to end up facing each other, and I tug her into my arms, burying my face in her neck. How can this tiny woman make me feel so much? How is it that I feel as though I've known her for years? How do I tell her that after only six weeks of knowing her, she's reached her hands inside my chest and wrapped them around my heart?

I had a pretty good idea that I was falling in love with her before she left Florida five weeks ago. Since then, every day, she does something or says something that reminds me of why she's perfect to me. She asks about baseball, my family, my classes, and even my friends. We have meaningful conversations, and I've missed her. I knew she was important to me, but it wasn't until I opened the door to her parents' house earlier and laid eyes on her in person that I knew how important.

I'm in love with her.

I fell hard, and I fell fast, and I'm not scared of it. I know we're young and that us living so far apart will get harder before it gets better, but I know deep in my soul that it's all going to be worth it in the end.

"You good?" she asks.

Pulling back, I stare into her eyes. It's on the tip of my tongue to tell her, but I refrain. "I'm more than good."

"Thank you for coming all this way for one night."

"You don't have to thank me for coming to see you, Peyton."

"It's a long way for such a short amount of time. I was sad and even a little angry that I couldn't be with you today." She lifts her head to look at me. "You are the best present I've ever received."

I kiss her because what do I say to that other than I love you? I can't, and I'm afraid to tell her and scare her away, so a kiss it is.

"We'll take what we can get when we can get it," I assure her.

"This is hard, Griffin."

"Yeah," I agree.

"But I'd rather be like this than not have you at all. I can't…" She stops.

"What were you going to say?" I push her hair out of her eyes.

"I can't imagine my life without you in it."

"You don't have to. I'm right here. And when I'm not…" I place my hand over her heart. "I'm right here."

"Yeah," she agrees with a small smile. She places her head on my chest, and we drift off to sleep.

CHAPTER 17
Peyton

K ARINA IS STAYING WITH HER parents tonight, which means I have the apartment all to myself. Her grandma is visiting from out of town. I'll stop by there tomorrow to say hello, but I wanted to give them family time tonight. She argued that I was family, but to be honest, I just wanted to watch Griffin's game on TV and call it a night.

Unfortunately for me, that means I have to head to my parents' house. We don't get the college sports station showing his game, but they do. My dad gets every damn sports channel imaginable. I'm hoping I can sneak down to the basement and watch the game in peace and slip back out. I want to drool over my man in peace.

When I pull into the empty driveway, the house is dark, but I know my parents, and I'm not willing to risk walking in on something I shouldn't ever see. I should have texted my mom earlier, but I forgot. Pulling my phone out of my purse, I fire off a text.

Hey, I'm here. Are you all home?

Mom:

No, we went out to dinner. I wish I knew you were coming. I could have cooked, or you could have come with us.

I'm good. I want to watch Griffin's game tonight, but I don't have the channel. I know Dad gets all of them.

Mom:

You don't need to tell me why you're home, Peyton. It will always be your home if you are nineteen or ninety.

Love you. I'll be in the basement.

Mom:

Love you too.

Clutching my keys and my purse, I make my way into the house. I don't bother turning on any of the lights. Instead, I head downstairs and flip on the TV. The game starts right now, and I still have to find the channel. Reaching for my phone, I pull up my last message with Griffin, where he tells me what station. I find it easily and turn up the volume so I don't miss anything. Moving to the small kitchen area, I pop some popcorn and grab a Dr Pepper from the fridge.

My eyes have been glued to the screen every inning. Griffin has pitched a hell of a game so far. They're in the ninth inning, and he's still on the mound. His arm is fire tonight. He winds up the pitch, and the batter strikes out, and I cheer for him like I've been doing all night. I know he can't see me, but I can't help it.

"What's with all the ruckus?" Dad asks with a smile on his face. He plops down on the couch beside me and helps himself to some of the popcorn that I abandoned a few innings ago.

"Griff's pitching a great game," I tell him. I go on to give him some highlights, catching him up to speed.

Dad sits with me through the end of the game. "He's good," he comments. There's surprise in his voice.

"See, I told you he wasn't some cocky asshole."

"Lady," he warns, and I stick my tongue out at him. I'm nineteen, and I can cuss if I want. I open my mouth to tell him just that, but the reporter on the TV says Griffin's name and pulls my attention away from my father.

"I'm Tiffany Banks, and I'm here with freshman Griffin Anthony. Great game out there, Griffin. How's the arm?"

He smiles. "Thanks, Tiffany. The arm is great." He smiles, and I can imagine everyone there seeing his pearly whites on the jumbotron and swooning just like I am sitting here in the basement next to my dad.

"You seem laser-focused out there tonight. Care to tell us what your secret is?" Tiffany, the reporter, asks him.

"She's no secret," he tells her.

"She?"

"My girlfriend, Peyton. I know she's at home in Nashville watching me tonight, and well, I guess this game is for her." He looks away from Tiffany and stares into the camera. "I miss you, babe. I'll be calling you as soon as I can get to my phone." He winks, and I swear I feel like my heart will pound out of my chest and the butterflies in my belly are going to wreak havoc.

"Lady, look at you," Dad says softly. "You're glowing."

"He's so good to me, Dad. I know the long distance will be hard, and I'm not sure if that's why you don't like him, but we're making this work. I really care about him."

"I can see that." He puts his arm around my shoulders and pulls me into a hug. "It's not the long distance that bothers me. Both of your sisters and even your mother and me had to do something similar."

"Then what is it?"

"Nothing," he admits. "There is nothing that I can find wrong with him. I tried to make him uncomfortable, but he stood his ground, which I'm sure you've seen."

"Yep. Parker even sent me the video," I tell him.

"I just have a hard time with my girls growing up. As the youngest, you're my baby, and I thought I had more time before someone took you away from me."

"He's not taking me away, Dad."

"I know that too." He grins. "But I liked being the only man in your life. All of your lives, and I know that this is the progression of life, but I don't have to like it."

"You've adjusted well with Cameron and even Holden. Just wait. In a few years, you'll have a house full of grandkids to spoil, and you'll be glad we all found men who will love us the way that you love Mom."

"Do you love him, lady?"

"I do. He doesn't know that yet, but I do."

He nods. "Then you have to follow your heart, but he needs to remember that I loved you first."

"You can tell him that when you see him."

"I think I will." He laughs. "Come on, let's go say hi to your mom." He stands and offers me his hand to help me off the couch. I fold the blanket I was using and clean up my mess before following him upstairs to see my mom before heading back to my apartment.

"You killed it!" I tell Griffin a couple of hours later on the phone.

"Thanks, babe."

"I saw that interview too." I toss that out there.

"I was hoping you would."

"I'm excited that I get to come and see you this weekend. My game should be over around three on Friday, and my flight leaves at six."

"Are you sad the season is over?"

"Yes and no. I hate that we lost more than we won, but we're a young team."

"You'll get them next year."

"Maybe. Maybe not. It doesn't hold the strong appeal as it did when I was younger. I love it, don't get me wrong, and the sport will always be in my blood, but I have no plans to pursue it after college."

"You're close to the team, though, right?"

"Kind of. They all know my family, or who my family is rather. They're all fake as hell, if I'm being honest. I hate that. I just want to be me."

"I'm sorry."

"It is what it is. But you. You and your team are kicking ass. I'm excited to get to see you play."

"Me too. Although, I just hope I can focus knowing you're in the stands watching." He chuckles. "Did Karina decide if she's coming with you?"

"She's not. Not this time. She said she doesn't want to be the third wheel."

"Ollie will be around. You know he's into her, right?"

"Oh, I know. She's into him too, but neither of them has confessed yet."

"I'll have to tell him he needs to put it out there."

"They'll figure it out. We did."

"I guess you're right," he agrees.

"Why do three weeks seem longer than five?" I ask him.

"I miss you too," he replies.

"You sound beat."

"I am, but I want to watch a movie with you."

"We don't have to. Get some rest. You pitched one hell of a game and with no relief. I know you're exhausted."

"Peyton, yes, I'm tired, but baby, I'm never too tired to spend time with you," he says over a yawn.

"Good night, Griffin," I say sweetly. "Just two more days and I'm hopping on a plane to see you. I need to pack anyway."

"Okay. I can't wait to see you."

"Me too. Night."

"Night."

Ending the call, I get to work packing my bag. I'm skipping classes on Monday and Tuesday to stay and watch his game. It's the first one I'll be able to watch in person. Then I'll fly home on Tuesday late afternoon. My grades are good, and I'm bringing what I need to study while I'm there for my finals in two weeks. I'll get to spend three full days with him, other than when he's at practice, and I can't wait. Saturday night is his parents' wedding anniversary, and we're taking them to dinner. Other than that, he's all mine.

"You about ready to head out?" I ask Karina. It's Friday morning, and we're heading to our game. It's rare that we have games on Friday, but this is the last game of the season, and it's almost as if it was added to the schedule as an afterthought.

"Yes. Five minutes," she calls back as there's a knock on the door.

"Are you expecting anyone?" I ask, walking past her room to get to the door.

"No. Why? Is someone here?"

"Yeah, well, I think so." I laugh. "I'm pretty sure I heard a knock." Pulling open the door, I stand frozen. "Am I dreaming?"

Griffin laughs. "You're not dreaming."

That pulls me out of my trance, and I rush him, jumping into his arms. He catches me with ease, just like I knew he would.

"Don't mind me," Oliver jokes.

"Hi, Ollie." I lift my head and wave at him.

"Where is she?"

"In her room." He nods and heads that way.

"What are you doing here?"

"I couldn't go all season and not watch one of your games. We decided late last night. We rented a car, and here we are."

"But I fly out today," I remind him.

"I know. I got ahold of your sisters, and they helped move your flight so that we could fly back together. Our flight leaves at nine now, and we're having dinner with your family after the game."

Hot tears prick my eyes. "I can't believe you're here." I lean in and press my lips to his.

"What's better is now we get more time together."

"More than you think," I confess.

"How so?" He steps into our apartment, shuts the door, and carries me to the couch, sitting down with me straddling his lap.

"I'm staying for your game on Monday. My flight leaves late Tuesday."

"What?" he asks. His face lights up. "Fuck, Peyton. I feel like it's Christmas," he says, placing his hands on my cheeks and kissing me soundly.

"I want to see you play in person. You only have a few weeks left of your season, so it makes sense to make it happen this trip," I confess.

"Great minds and all that." He smiles.

"Ollie?" I ask.

"He's staying here. His flight is early Sunday morning. He's making his move."

"Wow."

"Yep."

"I need to get going."

"Come on. I need to watch my girl kick ass on the field." Another quick kiss to my lips, and we stand just as Oliver and Karina come out of her room. They're holding hands, and she's biting down on her bottom lip, trying not to smile.

"Ready?" I ask her.

"Yes."

The drive to the field is short. When we get there, Oliver and Griffin insist on carrying our bags even though we can manage on our own. Who says chivalry is dead? As we're walking into the stadium, Griffin freezes.

"Coach?"

"Griff, Ollie." He nods. "I thought I might run into you here."

"Sir, you gave us the time off," Oliver says, making him laugh.

"I did. I also figured this one," he points at Griffin, "would be coming to see his girl. Our softball coach was coming and asked me if I wanted to tag along."

"Coach, this is my girlfriend, Peyton Monroe," Griffin introduces. He looks down at me. "Babe, this is Coach Hopkins."

"It's nice to meet you." I offer him my hand.

"You as well. This one tells me you're a beast on the field. His words, not mine," Coach says, pointing at Griffin.

"I think he's a little biased," I reply nervously.

"And this is my girl, Karina. Karina, this is Coach Hopkins," Oliver introduces.

I look over at my best friend, and her face is bloodred. "It's nice to meet you," she says politely, offering him her hand.

"I hate to be rude, but we really need to go," I tell them.

Griffin ignores everyone around us and bends his head to kiss me. "Good luck, babe."

"Thank you. I'll see you after the game. Coach Hopkins, it was nice to meet you," I say, remembering my manners as Karina and I take our bags from the guys and jog off to the locker room.

CHAPTER 18
Griffin

B Y THE TIME OUR FLIGHT lands, it's late, and we're both exhausted. We both dozed on the plane, but I'm more than ready to curl up next to her and fall asleep with her in my arms. I can't stop my smile when I think about the fact that I get to do that very thing for the next four nights.

"Peyton, it's so good to see you," Mom gushes as she steps forward and pulls her into a hug.

"You too, Mrs. Anthony."

"Anna," Mom corrects her.

"How was your flight?" Dad asks, pulling Peyton into a hug as soon as Mom releases her.

"It was good," we both say at the same time.

"Thank you for picking us up," Peyton tells them.

"Of course, let's get you home. I'm sure you're both exhausted. Griff said you won your game today," Mom says. She and Peyton walk ahead of us and chat about her game.

"This the only bag?" Dad asks.

"Yeah, I didn't take one. I knew we were coming back tonight, and she's only here for a few days."

"That's tough," he says, taking Peyton's bag and placing a hand on my shoulder. "We better get moving before we lose sight of them."

"Yeah, that's not happening," I say as my feet start to move. "She's here until Tuesday late afternoon, and I don't plan on letting her out of my sight until then."

"Oh, so I guess this is a bad time to tell you that your mother and I talked about it, and we think Peyton should stay in the spare bedroom."

"What?" I stop walking to look at him.

"We think it's best."

I can't believe this. They know what she means to me, and I'm an adult. We both are. If I want her in my bed next to me, that shouldn't be an issue. Fuck that. No way is she sleeping across the hall from me. If I saw her every day, maybe I might let that go, but my time with her is sacred and limited, and I'm not wasting a fucking second. Instead of arguing with him, I pull my phone from my pocket and begin to look for a room for us for the next four nights.

"What are you doing?" Dad asks. "They're getting ahead of us."

"I'm booking us a room," I tell him.

"What?"

"Look, Dad. I get it that it's your house and all that, but I'm not going to have her sleeping down the hall when she can be sleeping in my arms. It's not going to happen." I don't bother telling him that we've never, that I've never, had actual intercourse before in my life. It doesn't matter. All that matters is her in my arms. I'll do what I have to do to make that happen.

"Stop." Dad places his hand over mine. I look up at him, and he's smiling.

"What are you smiling about? You know how hard this is being away from her, and now you do this?" I'm pissed, and he knows it. His smile grows, and it makes me want to punch something. Not him, but something.

"I was teasing, Griff. Your mother and I know you're in love with this girl. There's no other reason you'd put yourself through this if you didn't. We like Peyton, and your mom changed the sheets on your bed earlier today. It's ready for both of you."

"That's wrong, old man." I point at him. My shoulders sag as some of the tension drains from my body. Looking down at my phone, I was just about ready to hit the Book Now button. I contemplate doing it anyway to give us some privacy, but I want her to spend time with my family too.

"I'm sorry. I didn't think I was that convincing." He laughs.

I slide my phone in my back pocket as we begin walking again. "We don't joke about Peyton. Not ever."

He nods, his lips tilted in a grin. "You remind me of me when I was your age. When I met your mother, I knew I would do whatever it took to make her mine and keep it that way."

"You were in college, right?"

"Freshman year, just like you. Here we are all those years later."

"Slowpokes!" Mom calls out.

I glance up to see Peyton smiling and laughing with my mom. Her eyes meet mine, and it's as if her smile is reaching into my chest and squeezing my heart. I've never loved anything or anyone the way that I love Peyton. Now, I just need to find the courage to tell her and hope it doesn't scare her away.

"Are you sure your parents are okay with us being in the same room?" she asks.

"Trust me. They're fine with it. Mom even changed the sheets knowing you were coming," I tell Peyton that same thing Dad told me at the airport.

"Okay." She yawns. "I'm going to change and call it a night. I'm exhausted."

"No clothes."

"But your parents," she counters.

"We'll lock the door, but baby, you're here for four nights, and I need to feel you next to me. I'll let you sleep, I promise. I just want to hold you."

"How am I supposed to say no to that?"

"You're not." I come around the bed and kiss the top of her head. "Go do what you have to do, but come back to me naked."

"So bossy." She turns to walk into the bathroom connected to my bedroom, but I grab her wrist to stop her.

"I will never force you to do anything you don't want to do. If you really want to wear clothes, you can." I swallow back the lump in my throat. I want to demand that she's naked anytime we're alone, but I don't have the right. She's mine, but she's also her own person.

She turns and slides her hands behind my neck and peers up at me. "I trust you, Griff. I know you would never pressure me. In fact, I kind of like the way you get a little bossy. It shows me that you want me."

"There will never be a day when I have breath in my lungs that I don't want you. Maybe not even after that."

"Thousands of butterflies," she whispers.

"What?"

"That's what it feels like in my belly when you say things like that. Thousands of butterflies."

"Good." I kiss her quickly and step out of her hold. "Go do what you need to do. It's been too damn long since I've held you all night, and just so you know, we're sleeping in tomorrow."

She spins on her heels and heads toward the bathroom. I lock my bedroom door and shut off the light, bathing the room in darkness before stripping naked and sliding under the covers.

"Yikes, I can't see you." She laughs.

"Just follow my voice. It's a straight shot to the bed, and there is nothing in your way."

"Okay." I hear her moving toward me, and when she reaches the bed, I hold the covers up. "Come here."

The bed dips as she climbs in beside me. Draping the cover over us, I pull her into my arms and close my eyes. "This is where you belong."

"You think so?"

"I know so." I press my lips to the crown of her head. "Thank you for coming this weekend. I know today was a long day for you."

"Not just me. You drove all night to get to me."

"Worth every mile."

She settles in close, and I breathe her in. I know I said that we could do this long-distance stuff, and I still believe that, but I don't want to. I want to be with her like this every damn day. If I ever get drafted, I'll spend a lot of time away from her, and something just tells me that I need to soak up as much time with her as I possibly can.

"What are you thinking about?" she asks.

"What makes you think I'm thinking about something?"

"You're tense."

"I've been thinking. I'm going to talk to Coach Hopkins about helping me transfer to Nashville."

"What?" She sits up, and even though it's dark, I can feel her gaze.

"I don't want to be away from you, Peyton. I hate this."

"Maybe we should," she starts, but somehow in the dark, I manage to place my hand over her mouth.

"If you were going to say we should take a break, or step back, or break up, or whatever thing in your head that has us not being together... don't. None of those things are options."

"You can't give up your full ride, and you were the starting pitcher as a freshman, Griff. That's a big deal. And what about the draft? Do you know how rare it is not to have to go to the farm team first, and they're talking about bringing you straight on. There are tons of teams looking at you, even your grandpa's favorite team, the Mavericks. I won't let you give all of that up for me."

"I love that you listen to me. I love that I can have a conversation with you about my future and know that you're really hearing me. I love that you're as invested in my dreams as I am. Babe, if it's meant to be, it will be."

"You could say the same about us."

"No, Peyton. I can't say that. You see, if college is my last run at playing the game I love, I'll be fine. I have two degrees to fall back on. I'll be okay. I can live a full, happy life without the game, but I can't do that without you."

"You can't say things like that." Her voice cracks.

"I'm being honest with you. I'm sorry if that bothers you." Even I can hear the anguish in my tone, and I hate that. I love baseball, but I love her more. The anguish isn't from the loss of the sport I love. It's the thought of losing her that gets me.

"No. It doesn't, but it makes me fall further in love with you, and I don't know how to handle that."

"What?" I ask.

"I don't know how to handle it when you say those things."

"I heard that part. What about the part before it?"

"I can't say it again," she says softly.

"Why?"

"Because I didn't mean to say it then, and now you're probably ready to kick me out of your bed and run for the hills."

"Do you really think that?"

"No. But I didn't mean to just blurt it out like that."

I move us so that I'm hovering over her. I wish I could see her face, but I know by the way her arms wrap around my biceps and the hitch in her breath that I have her attention. "I love you. I love you so much that I can't stand the thought of you getting on that plane in a few days and going back to Tennessee without me. I know I said we could do this, and I still believe we can, but I don't want to. I want to walk you to class and have lunch with you. I want to settle in bed with you just like this at the end of every day. I want to start my day the same."

"I love you too. I want that. All of that, but I don't see how we can make it work. I won't let you give up what you're building here."

"I don't care about that. Your school has a great men's baseball team. The scouts and my reputation and skill for the game can follow me there."

"You have a full ride, Griff. That's a big deal. You're the starting pitcher. That's an even bigger deal. You could lose that status and hurt your chances to be drafted."

"My parents have a college fund for me, and I have my inheritance."

"That's for you to start your life, not sink it into college when you're already getting it paid for."

"That's exactly what I'll be doing. Starting my life. With you."

"We're both tired, and it's been a long day. Can we talk about this tomorrow?"

"Sure, but I'm not going to change my mind." Dipping my head, I kiss down her chest, pulling a hard nipple into my mouth.

"You aren't going to persuade me like that," she pants.

I release her nipple with an audible pop and roll over, pulling her back to my front. "Not tonight. I know you're exhausted, and I'm running on fumes. We can pick that up in the morning, as well as our conversation."

She snuggles into my embrace, and I hold her tighter. We're both quiet, and I'm pretty sure she's already fallen asleep by the way her breathing has evened out. I close my eyes, savoring the fact that she's here, and at this moment, I know I've made my choice.

I choose her.

Whatever I have to do to have this every day of forever, I'm willing to make it happen.

"I want it all too," she whispers. "I would give anything to be with you like this every day."

"Every day of forever," I reply softly.

"I love you, Griff."

"Love you too, baby." Those are our last spoken words as we both drift off to sleep.

CHAPTER 19
Peyton

I'VE BEEN LYING AWAKE WELL before the sun rose in the sky. I made sure to stay still and not wake Griffin. He had a long day yesterday and needs his sleep. I was content to lie here in his arms and let my mind drift to our conversation last night. I can't believe that I blurted out that I'm in love with him.

He loves me too.

When I feel his lips press against my bare shoulder, I smile. He's awake. "Morning, sleepyhead."

"How long have you been up?"

"A few hours."

"Hours? Why didn't you wake me?"

I roll over and snuggle into his chest. "Because you drove all night long to watch my last game of the season. Because you flew home with me and held me in your arms all night long. Because I love you, and I wanted to make sure you were rested."

He grins a boyish grin. "I wasn't dreaming, huh?" he asks.

"Dreaming about what?"

"You telling me that you love me."

"No. You weren't dreaming," I tell him as his phone vibrates on the nightstand.

Groaning, he rolls over and grabs his phone. "It's my dad," he tells me before answering. "Hey, what's up?" he asks, his voice still laced with sleep. His eyes brighten. "Really? She's going to love that." He nods. "Okay, we'll get ready and be down." He ends the call and drops the phone onto the bed beside him.

"Everything okay?"

"Yeah. Dad actually made a last-minute decision to take Mom away for the night. He said that we inspired him."

"We did?" I ask, confused.

"Apparently, he's going to take her back to their old college town in Ohio. That's where they met. Their flight leaves this afternoon."

"So, no dinner with them tonight?"

"No. Breakfast instead. Dad said it will be ready in thirty minutes."

"Eeep." I toss off the covers and climb out of bed, rushing to my bag.

"Want some company?"

"No. If you do that, we're never going to make it downstairs for breakfast."

"I think they'll understand." He winks.

"No, Griffin, this is their wedding anniversary. I'll be quick," I say, disappearing into the bathroom with my bag. I turn the lock on the door just in case. It's not that I don't trust him. It's that I don't trust myself with him. He's too damn tempting.

Thirty minutes later, we walk hand in hand to the kitchen. Anna is sitting at the island with a steaming cup of coffee in her hands while Gary flips pancakes on the griddle.

"It smells delicious," I tell him. "Happy anniversary." I give his mom a hug, and Gary gives me a huge smile.

"Thank you," he says. "Have a seat. Griff, get your girl something to drink. We're almost ready to eat."

Once we're all seated around the island, Gary reaches under the bowl of fruit and produces a card that he hands to Anna. "Happy anniversary," he tells her.

"Should I wait?"

"Never. Open it."

All eyes are on her as she opens the card. I watch as she reads what's inside and looks up at her husband with tears in her eyes.

"You can thank the kids for this one," Gary tells her. "Seeing them together brings back some good memories."

"Are we really going back? When?"

"We're really going back, and our flight leaves in a few hours."

"But we had dinner plans. Peyton came all this way."

"Mom, Peyton isn't going anywhere. There will be more dinners and more anniversaries for her to celebrate with us."

She loses her battle with her tears as one slides down her cheek. "You remind me so much of your father." She wipes her cheeks.

"What can I do?" I ask her. "Do you need help packing?"

"Yes. I would love that. Right after breakfast. You don't want to miss Gary's pancakes, trust me."

I nod and cut a bite of my pancakes, and she's right. "Oh." I cover my mouth with my hand. "So good," I say once I've swallowed.

"Thank you."

"Dad makes them for all special occasions."

"I love that." I dive in for another bite as Gary and Anna take turns telling us stories about when they met. Griffin keeps one hand on my thigh the entire time. I feel as though I've been here before and known them all for years. They're always more than welcoming, and I couldn't ask for anything more.

"Right, it's time to pack," Anna says, standing. She takes her plate to the sink. I push back from the counter to do the same, but Griffin stops me.

"I'll get it." He leans in and kisses me. Just a quick peck, but I feel the heat rise to my cheeks, knowing he did so in front of his parents.

"Ready?" Anna asks.

"Absolutely." I follow her up to their bedroom and take a seat on their bed.

"I can't believe he's doing this," she gushes. "We have so many memories there."

"It's very sweet. What can I help with?"

"Honestly, just the company is great. When you've been married as long as I have, you don't worry about what you're wearing as much as when you first meet."

"I get that, but it might be fun to surprise him. Maybe break out something you haven't worn in a while."

"Oh, I have some lingerie I bought a few years ago on a whim, and I've never worn it."

"There you go."

"You're a genius. No wonder my son loves you." She laughs as she places a small suitcase on the bed and begins to add clothes to it.

It's a wonder that my heart even fits in my chest, with all the love that's bursting inside me. "I love him too," I confess with a whisper.

"Oh, honey, of course you do. Anyone who sees the two of you together can figure that out." She offers me a smile before saying, "I think I have it all," and glancing around her room.

"Cell phone charger?" I ask.

"Oh yes, I'll need that for sure." She goes to the nightstand, unplugs her charger, and tosses it into her suitcase.

"All set?" Gary asks. I turn to look, and he and Griffin are standing in the doorway.

"Yes. Are you packed?"

He grins, and it reminds me so much of his son. "I packed last night while you were in the tub."

"Sneaky." She goes to him and kisses him.

"That's why you love me." He grins. "Now, get your bag so we can head out. I hate having to rush through the airport."

"Okay. I think I have everything." Anna comes back to the bed and wraps her arms around me. "Thank you for your help. I'm sorry we're going to miss you while you're here."

"I'm actually staying until Tuesday afternoon. I decided to skip a couple of days of classes now that the season is over so that I can see Griffin's game."

"That's perfect. We're coming back when?" She turns to look at Gary.

"We're flying home Monday morning, so we can be here for the game as well."

"Good. You won't have to sit alone." She gives me another hug, moves to the door, and does the same to Griffin.

I stand and follow them out of the room. Griffin and I walk back downstairs with them, and stand on the front porch waving goodbye.

"What do you want to do today?" he asks.

"I'm up for anything. What did you have planned?"

"I thought we'd maybe go to the beach before meeting my parents for dinner, but Dad changed that. We have the house all to ourselves all weekend."

"So that means no beach?"

"Do you want to go to the beach?" he asks, sliding his arm around my waist and pulling me into his chest.

"I want to be where you are."

"I like the idea of locking ourselves inside or out back in the pool. Now that I know it can happen, I want you all to myself."

"I can get on board with that."

"Did you bring your suit?"

"Yep."

"Good. Let's go get changed, and we'll soak up some of that Florida sun you seem to love so much."

"Sounds good to me." Hand in hand, we make our way inside and up to his room to change.

I don't know how long we've been sitting out by the pool when my phone rings. Keeping my eyes closed behind my sunglasses, I reach for it on the table between the two lounge chairs and squint to swipe at the screen. "Hello?"

"Are you soaking up the sun?" Karina asks.

"You know it."

"I'm jealous. It's raining here today."

"You were invited to come with me."

"I know. I didn't expect him to show up here and stay."

"I've been trying to tell you that he's into you."

"Yeah, I kinda figured that out when he asked me to go out with him."

"What did you tell him?"

"That I didn't think I could do long distance like you and Griffin do."

"You can."

"I know, but I don't know if I want to."

"That's only a choice that you can make."

"Yeah. I really like him."

"Then go for it. You don't want to have any regrets."

"I'm thinking about it. Anyway, what time is dinner?"

"Change of plans, Gary took Anna back to their college stomping grounds for the weekend. They'll be back on Monday."

"So it's just you and Griffin for the rest of the weekend?"

"Tragic."

Her laughter fills my ears. "I'll let you go. Oliver's in the shower. I just wanted to check in with you."

"All good, and Karina, follow your heart. It may be the best choice you ever made, and it may end in heartbreak, but at least you'll have no regrets."

"Do you have regrets?"

I glance over at Griffin, who is stretched out on the lounge chair next to me, sleeping. "Not one."

"Thanks, Peyton. I'll call you later."

"Have fun."

"You too," she says.

I place my phone back on the table and stand from my chair. I settle next to Griffin on his. "My girlfriend's gonna kick your ass," he says huskily.

"Oh, yeah? I think I can take her."

He wraps his arms around me. "Sorry I fell asleep."

"It's fine. I was dozing off too. Karina called and woke me up."

"Everything good there?" he asks.

"Yeah. I guess Oliver asked her to try a long-distance relationship, and she's not sure she wants to do that."

"Sounds like he needs to be more convincing."

"Like you were? I remember you telling me you weren't going to let me on the plane unless I agreed to keep in touch."

"And look at us now." He grins, kissing my cheek. "It's hot as hell. You want to go for a swim?"

"Yes." He moves quickly and has me in his arms. "Griffin! You better not be tossing me into that pool," I warn.

"Not this time," he says. He walks us to the steps and carries me into the water. I move to where my legs are around his waist and my arms around his neck. He walks us deeper into the water, where nothing but our heads are above water.

"Thank you."

"You're welcome. But I did have an ulterior motive."

"What's that?"

"Getting you wrapped around me like this."

"I can't believe we're here." I hug him tighter. "It's so nice not to have to rush off and only have a few hours with you."

"Agreed. After we get cooled off, we should make some lunch."

"Babe, it's almost four. We've been out here for a while."

"No wonder I'm starving. Okay, so dinner."

"Then what?"

"Movie night? Where we get to watch with me holding you and not my computer."

"I can get on board with that," I tell him.

"Yeah?"

"Uh-huh."

"I've fucking missed you," he says before his lips crash with mine. I can feel his hard length between us as his tongue explores my mouth. His hands are gripping the back of my thighs, and even though there is very little clothing between us, it's still too much.

"Inside," I manage to say between kisses.

He pulls back from the kiss, his chest rising and falling at a rapid pace as he pulls air into his lungs. "Inside?"

"Not out here."

Understanding crosses his face, and he moves us to the steps. He doesn't put me down until we reach the lounge chairs so we can gather our phones and towels to bring them inside. With his hand on the small of my back, he guides me to the back door.

The air-conditioning hits, causing a chill to race over my body. "I'll warm you up," he says, his lips next to my ear. He trails kisses down my neck, driving me crazy.

"You hungry?" he asks.

"Yes."

"What sounds good?"

"You."

"Me?" He smiles.

"With a side of you."

"Do you know how much I love you?"

"If your heart is beating as fast as mine right now, I do."

He grabs my hand and places it over his heart. "It only beats this way for you."

"I need you."

"I'm right here." The next thing I know, he's lifting me in the air and tossing me over his shoulder as he makes his way up the stairs and to his room. My laughter bounces off the walls as he takes the steps two at a time.

CHAPTER 20
Griffin

M AKING IT TO MY ROOM, I kick the door closed behind me and move to lay Peyton on my bed. She's so damn beautiful. It takes my breath away to look at her. Her hair is fanned out over my pillow, and her tiny purple bikini easily shows me the curves of her body.

"Griff?" She holds her hand out for me. "You all right?"

"I don't know," I confess.

"Talk to me."

"My palms are sweaty," I say, placing my hand in hers. "My heart is beating so hard I fear it could beat right out of my chest." She moves to sit up and places the hand I'm not holding over my heart. "My knees are trembling, and my cock is so hard it hurts."

"It's just me." She smiles softly, and that gesture reaches into my chest and grabs my heart.

"That's just it, baby. It is you. You're the reason for all of it. I've never felt any of this before, not all at once."

"I feel it too," she confesses.

My hands move to her face, and she tilts her head back. I study her closely. I never want to forget this moment. The love I see in her eyes is shining so clearly, and it's all for me.

"Griffin?"

I have to swallow to get past the lump in my throat before I can speak. "Yeah?"

She doesn't say anything. Instead, her hands move to my swim trunks. I look between us and watch as she unties the strings and gives them a tug, causing them to fall to the floor. She takes my cock in her hand and strokes.

"Fuck," I mutter under my breath. My balls are already tight and heavy, and when she leans forward and takes me into her mouth, my eyes roll back in my head. I grip my hands at my sides, grappling for control, but it's not working. Her mouth is too hot and too wet, and if she doesn't stop, I'm going to come down her throat. That can't happen.

She comes first.

I take a step back, and my cock falls from her mouth with an audible pop. She wipes her mouth with the back of her hand, and there is a question in her eyes.

"I'm not coming before you do."

She smiles. "This isn't a contest, Griff."

"No. This is us, baby, and you come first."

"Well, you better get busy then," she sasses.

Before the words are even out of her mouth, I'm making quick work of shedding her of her purple bikini. "It looked great on you, but it looks better on my floor," I tell her, palming her breasts and tracing her nipples with my thumbs.

"Lie back." She does as I ask, her hair once again fanned out across my pillow. I climb onto the bed and lie next to her.

Propping myself up on my elbow, I let my free hand explore her. I start by tracing her lips with the pad of my thumb, letting my hand trail down her neck and to her chest.

I take my time cupping her breasts and tweaking her nipples with my thumb and index finger, making sure I give them both equal amounts of attention. She squirms, and her chest is rapidly rising and falling, but neither of us says a word.

My hand travels over her quivering belly until I reach her pussy. My thumb rolls over her clit, causing her to moan. I slide my fingers through her folds, and she's soaked. A few more strokes, and I'm sliding a finger inside her.

"I want you to feel this," I tell her.

"W-What?"

"Your pussy. I want you to feel what I feel."

"I did... that day on the video call."

"I know, but now you're here with me. I get to see up close and personal the flush of your skin and watch the rapid rise and fall of your chest with each breath. I can smell you all around me, while I watch you. Give me your hand." I remove mine from her body and reach for hers.

"Griffin?"

"I want to watch you in person." Together we move her hand between her thighs. I assist her with tracing her folds and then sliding her finger inside herself.

"Oh," she says as her eyes close.

"You're so warm and so wet. When you come, your walls tighten, and your body squeezes," I tell her.

She's slowly pumping her fingers, and my cock is weeping to feel her. Instead, I go for the next best thing and move my hand to rest over hers, sliding a long digit inside her, matching her rhythm.

"Griff..." My name is a plea falling from her lips. She arches her back off the bed, pushing her tits into the air. I capture one hard peak in my mouth and suck gently before nipping her with my teeth, only to soothe the ache with my tongue.

"I need—" She starts but doesn't finish what she was going to say.

"Tell me what you need, baby."

"I need to come. I just can't... I need something more."

Removing my finger from her pussy, she cries out in protest. Gently, I tug on her hand and bring it to my lips. I suck on her finger and mine, tasting her. Her taste explodes on my tongue, and I need more. Dropping our hands, I move to settle between her thighs. I lift her legs over my shoulders and get to work. I devour her with my mouth while she buries her hands in my hair.

"I can't. Griffin, I can't. It's too much," she pants.

She says the words, but her legs tighten around my head, holding me to her. She's close. I double down licking and sucking until she cries out my name. I don't stop until her hold on me eases and her grip on my hair falls away.

Slowly, I kiss my way up her body, lying next to her and pulling her into my arms. She's slick with sweat, and her breathing is labored while her heart races. I can feel it as I hold her against me.

"I love you, Griffin."

My heart soars. "I love you too." I know without a shadow of a doubt that there will never be a day where I won't mean that. There will never be a day moving forward where she's not the one who owns my heart.

Her hand finds its way between us, and she grips my cock. "Your turn," she purrs.

"That's not how this works," I tell her.

"That's how it works today," she tells me.

"Let me hold you."

"You have all night to hold me. Right now, I want to return the favor."

She doesn't realize that what we just shared was as much for me as it was for her. "You're a gift," I tell her.

She smiles and pushes on my shoulder, so I'm lying flat on my back. She straddles my hips, and I can feel her juices as they drop on my cock. She moves her hips back just enough that she can stroke me from root to tip, spreading her all over me.

My hands grip her hips as I try like hell to let her do her thing. She strokes me with both hands, and it takes every ounce of power I have not to close my eyes. I don't want to miss this.

"Griffin?"

"Hmm?"

"I want more."

"More of what?"

"More of you. More of this." She glances down to where my cock is double fisted in her hands.

I sit up, causing her to break her hold, and wrap her arms around me. "You have all of me," I tell her, brushing her hair out of her eyes.

"Not yet, but I want to."

"Pey—" I start, but her finger to my lips hushes me.

"I want you to make love to me."

My heart stalls, and it's several long seconds before it begins beating again. I swallow hard. I don't know what to say to that. I want to toss her on the bed and slide deep inside her and never leave, but this... *this* is a big deal for both of us.

"Maybe you should think about it," I tell her. It's not that I don't want to. I do, and I know she's it for me, but I don't want her making this choice in the heat of the moment, no matter how angry my cock will be for denying him entry to the promised land.

"I have thought about it. I wasn't waiting for marriage, but I was waiting for you."

"We can't," I say with a sigh. "I don't have protection. I wasn't planning on this."

"Lucky for you, I was." She grins as she climbs off my lap and off the bed. She moves to her bag that's resting on the floor and digs around inside. She lifts a new box of condoms in the air, and the smile on her face, one of victory and desire, is one I will never forget as long as I live.

On her way back to the bed, she tears open the box and breaks off a small foil packet, placing the remainder on the nightstand. She hands it to me, then climbs back on the bed and lies on her back. "I think... like this," she says, her face blushing.

Now she chooses to get all bashful on me?

"I think you on top, you know, for the first time, would be better."

"Are you sure about this?"

"The only other thing that I'm more sure of is how much I love you."

Damn. Her words hit me in the feels. Sitting back on my knees, I tear open the condom. My hands shake as I roll the latex over my hard length. Tossing the wrapper to the floor, I hover over her and settle my weight on my elbows on either side of her head. My cock is nestled against her pussy, and my heart is banging against my rib cage like a drum.

She lifts her hands to rest on either side of my face. "I want this, Griffin. I want you."

"Me too," I whisper. There's a crack in my voice.

"What's going on in that head of yours?" she inquires.

"Love. So much love, and I'm trying to memorize every touch, every breath of this moment."

"This isn't a one and done."

I nod. "It's the last piece of me I have to give you. You have all of me, Peyton."

"And you have all of me. Well, almost, there's this one little thing," she says, wrapping her legs around my waist.

"I don't want to hurt you."

"You'd never hurt me. This will be painful, but I know I'm safe with you. I know that you're going to take care of me. This is something we only get to give away once. I want it to be you."

"I want it to be you." I echo her words.

No more words are spoken as I slowly push my hips forward. She sucks in a breath but urges me to keep going, so I do. Inch by inch, I move forward.

"Just do it," she says, panting.

"I'm sorry," I say as I push all the way in one thrust. White-hot heat courses through me. She's so damn tight and warm, my cock twitches. "Are you okay?"

She opens her eyes. "I'm okay. It wasn't as bad as I thought it would be."

"Tell me when I can move."

"You can move."

"Are you sure?" I hate the thought that this is hurting her when it feels so fucking incredible to me.

I pull almost all the way out and then push back in. I repeat this process a few times. I try to think about anything other than how unbelievable her pussy feels gripping my cock like a vise. I run through baseball stats in my head, but it's not working. She's too intoxicating.

"Touch yourself."

"What?"

"Babe, I'm close. I need you there. I'm on the verge of losing control."

"Then let go."

"You come first."

"I did." She grins.

"Then do it again. Touch yourself."

She slides her hand between us, and a throaty moan passes her lips. "Oh," she pants.

"Tell me what you need."

"Faster."

Doing as she asks, I increase my speed, all while still trying to think about baseball stats and not the beautiful woman beneath me.

"Right... there," she says, lifting her hips to meet me, thrust for thrust.

"Damn," I mutter as her pussy grips me even tighter.

"Oh. My. God."

"Open your eyes." Her lids flutter open. "I want to watch you when you fall over the edge."

"Griffin!" She shouts my name, and her pussy grips my cock.

I can't hold on a second longer as I release inside Peyton while she's gripping me. It's the best orgasm and most intimate moment of my life. I still as my release pulses inside. Once we're both drained, I lower myself to her, careful not to crush her, and take her lips with mine.

Her arms surround my neck, and she holds me close. "I love you, Griffin. I love you so much."

"I love you too." I pull back and kiss the tip of her nose. "I need to take care of the condom. I'll be right back." I hate to leave Peyton, her body, this bed, but I need to handle my business. In the bathroom, I clean up, tossing the condom in the trash, and grab a wet washcloth to clean her.

"Open for me," I say, sitting on the edge of the bed and tapping her thighs.

"What are you doing?"

"Taking care of you." Her eyes soften, and her legs fall open. I gently clean her up and toss the cloth through the bathroom door. I hear it land on the floor with a plop as I climb back into bed and pull her into my arms.

I don't have words to explain what I'm feeling. I don't know how to tell her what she means to me or thank her for the gift she just gave me. I've never been more glad of any decision in my life as I am that I waited for her.

"You'll always have a piece of me," she whispers.

"And you'll always have all of me," I counter. I hold her close as our breathing evens out, and we both fall fast asleep.

CHAPTER 21
Peyton

I DON'T WANT TO GO home. The thought is sobering and sad all at the same time. I miss my family, but this connection that I have with Griffin is... something I can't explain. It's almost as if we're tethered to each other. It's more than just the love I have for him. It's something more, something I can't decipher.

"Hey, are you Peyton Monroe?" a woman who just sat next to me in the stands asks.

"I am. And you are?"

"I'm Cecelia Stone." She offers me her hand.

Not wanting to be rude, I take her offered hand and shake. "Nice to meet you," I say politely. Partly because that's how I was raised, partly because Anna is sitting on my other side and Gary next to her. I don't want Griffin's parents to think I'm a bitch, and third is I don't know if this woman is anything to Griffin, and being rude to someone who could be connected to him wouldn't be cool of me.

"You're dating Griffin Anthony?" she asks.

"Who did you say you were again?" I ask. I stiffen my shoulders, preparing for what comes next, but it's not at all what I was expecting.

She smiles kindly. "I'm the head coach of the softball team." She points at her shirt, and I clearly see the logo for Griffin's college embroidered on the crest.

"I'm sorry. I'm just used to people realizing who my family is, and I get a little defensive at times."

"It's good not to let your guard down until you know what the situation is. There is no harm in that," she assures me.

"Yes, Griffin and I are dating."

"Long distance is hard."

"Sounds like you've done your homework."

"I have." She chuckles. "I've also seen you play. I was at your game on Friday."

"What?" I turn to look at her this time, giving her more of my attention. "Me and my assistant coach, Tom Wilson, as well as Griffin's coach, Fred Hopkins, we travel at times to scout players."

"From other colleges?" I ask. I remember Coach Hopkins telling us that the softball coach was there as well, but I didn't think anything of it.

"Sometimes, mostly high school, but we've been known to pick up a college game here and there. We saw Griffin in the stands cheering you on, and now here you are."

"I haven't been able to make it to one of his games all season, so I'm playing hooky for a few days to make this happen."

"Nothing wrong with a few mental health days now that the season is over." She winks.

"My thoughts exactly."

"Peyton, we're going to grab a drink. Would you like anything?" Anna asks.

"A bottle of water, please," I reach into my purse for money, and Gary waves me off.

"Your money is no good here." He laughs, taking his wife by the hand and leading her down the steps.

"Hanging out with the parents, I see."

This woman knows way more than I would expect her to know. "Yep."

"He looks good out there. Almost pitched a no-hitter."

"I know. But let's not talk about it. We have two more innings, and I don't want to jinx him."

"Got it. Look over to your right. There are two men in Ohio gear. They're from the majors. Rumor has it they're here to watch Griffin."

"Wow. Are you serious?" I casually look over and scan the crowd until I see the men she's referring to.

"Griffin has incredible talent on the field, and he's getting a lot of attention."

My heart swells. "I'm so excited for him."

"Are you?" she asks.

"Yes. Of course, I am. He's worked his ass off to be where he is. He gives everything to this sport he loves."

"He's lucky to have you."

"I'm the lucky one." I turn my attention back to the game. One more inning, and he's done it. Pitched a no-hitter.

"He's on fire tonight," Gary says, handing me a bottle of water.

"Thank you. He really is."

"He's showing off for you," Anna jokes.

"Nah, he's always this good."

"True," Gary agrees. "However, I do think that you give him some extra motivation." I can feel the flush of my cheeks as I imagine the extra motivation we've been giving each other. "I'm just here to support him."

"And he knows that. He knows you're here for him. Not what he can do on that field. That's pretty damn good motivation if you ask me," Gary states.

I smile at him and turn my attention back to the field. My leg bounces as I peel the label from my bottle of water. Two outs and another batter strolls up to the plate. I hold my breath as Griffin winds up the pitch and lets it fly. I watch as the ball reaches the plate and the batter swings.

"Strike!" the umpire calls out.

I stand, as do his parents, and even Coach Stone climbs to her feet. The anticipation of what's about to happen propels her to do so. Griffin winds up his second pitch, and I hold my breath until I hear, "Strike two!"

"Come on, baby," I say under my breath. I know he can't hear me, but maybe he will telepathically get the message that I'm standing here cheering him on.

Griffin glances into the stands, and I swear he's looking right at me. I mouth, "I love you," even though I know he can't see me, and hold my breath as he winds up the pitch and lets the ball fly.

"Sttrriiikkee three! You're out!" the umpire calls.

I jump up and down and hug his parents and even Coach Stone. "He did it. He did it." I clap and scream and cheer for my man, who has pitched his first no-hitter of his college career. The crowd roars around me, most of them chanting Griffin's name and calling out for him. I hear my name being called, but I don't know where it's from. I look all around, and it's Gary who points it out. Sam, Daniel, and Oliver are all in the dugout calling out to me. Once they see that they have my attention, they wave for me to come closer. I'm not sure why, but I do it anyway, taking the steps slowly until I reach them. "Hey, guys. Great game."

"Get over here," Sam says. Before I know what's happening, he has his hands on my waist, and he's lifting me over the wall.

"What are you doing?" I laugh.

"Go greet your man. You're his good luck charm."

"No. This is all Griffin. And I can't go out there. It's a mob."

"Fine." Daniel rolls his eyes. "The things we do for love." The next thing I know, he's nodding at Sam, and they're hoisting me onto their shoulders. Oliver laughs as he walks in front of them, clearing the path.

"This is crazy," I call out to them, but they don't seem to care that I'm even talking. Instead, they carry me effortlessly through the crowd, following Oliver and only stopping once they reach Griffin.

"Hey, Griff, we brought you something," Sam calls out to him.

"Or someone," Daniel corrects him.

Griffin's smile lights up his entire face as the guys lower me to the ground. Only to be picked up by Griffin as he spins me around. When he stops spinning us, I wrap my legs around his waist and kiss him soundly. "I'm so proud of you."

"You have to come to all of my games from now on." He laughs. "You're good luck."

"You don't need luck, Griffin. It's all you and your talent. Babe! You just pitched a no-hitter."

"And you were here to see it," he says, burying his face in my neck.

"Griffin, great game," a guy with a polo shirt representing one of the major sports networks tells him. He holds a microphone to his mouth and nods to the camera guy behind him. "Great game. How does it feel to pitch your first college no-hitter as a freshman?"

"It feels great." Griffin smiles.

I tap his shoulder, telling him silently to let me down, and he does. His eyes find mine as he slowly helps me slide down his body.

"Who's this?"

"This is my girlfriend. This is the first game she's been able to make this season because of her own softball schedule," he tells them.

"Sounds like she's your good luck charm." The reporter laughs.

Griffin leans down and kisses my forehead before turning back to the reporter. He adjusts his gaze to look at the camera. "She's my everything."

Several things happen at once. First, heat rushes to my core. Second, my heart trips over in my chest and expands with love for him. Third, the butterflies swarm, causing my belly to flutter, and fourth, he slides his hand behind my neck and kisses me.

On. National. Television.

I can only hope they edit this out. I can imagine what my dad is thinking right now if he's watching, and I'm certain he's watching. He knows I'm here, and Mom told me he's been recording all of Griffin's televised games so he can watch them. I know this isn't what he would be expecting to see on his TV screen.

His teammates descend on us, and the reporter gets pushed back from the chaos. Griffin ends the kiss and rests his forehead against mine. We're standing in the middle of the baseball field surrounded by his teammates, reporters, coaching staff, fans, fellow students, and I don't see or hear any of them. All I see is the man holding me as if I'm the most precious thing in his world.

"I love you." He smiles.

"I love you too."

He pulls me close and thrusts his fist in the air, celebrating with his teammates. Not once does he let go of me. This is his moment, his achievement, and he wants me here with him.

Clarity washes over me, and I know what I have to do. It's something that I've been considering for a while, and this moment gives me the answer I've been searching for.

"I need to go shower," Griffin says once the crowd has died down.

"Go. Do your thing. I'm going to find my way back to the bleachers and look for your parents."

"They're still in the same spot. Come on. I'll walk you over." Hand in hand, he leads me back to the dugout where Sam and Daniel lifted me over the wall. "Dad!" he calls out, and Gary turns immediately. Griffin waves him over. "I need an assist," he says.

Before I know what's going on, he's gripping my hips and lifting me into the air. Gary takes over, lifting me from his arms and setting me on my feet. "You two are too much." I laugh.

"Take care of my girl." Griffin points at his dad.

"Go." I shoo him away, laughing.

"Come on." Gary laughs, placing his arm around my shoulders. "We'll wait at our seats so he knows where to find us."

Anna is still sitting in the same place, chatting with Coach Stone. I take a seat next to them, just as Griffin's voice fills the stadium. My eyes move to the giant screens to see his smiling face in the locker room. Another reporter is interviewing him. He's humble and praises his team.

"And what about your good luck charm?"

He smiles, and my heart melts. "She's with my family, waiting on me." The reporter opens his mouth to ask more questions, but Sam appears on the screen, jumping onto Griffin's back, effectively ending the interview.

"Sounds like the two of you have something special," Coach Stone comments from her seat next to me.

"Yeah," I agree.

"Not many people can handle a long-distance relationship. Especially those as young as the two of you," she says.

"Well, I guess when you know, you know." I shrug.

She chuckles at my reply. "It's easy to see that you both care about each other."

"We do." I'm not sure what her angle is. It seems to be a little weird to have her talking about my relationship like this.

"Well, I'm going to head out. It was nice meeting you all." She offers me her hand, and I shake it. She then turns to Anna and Gary. "Your son is one hell of a ballplayer."

"Thank you," they reply.

With that, she turns and walks away. "She was kind of... weird," I tell Griffin's parents.

"How so?"

"She just kept talking about me and Griffin and how hard long-distance is, especially at our age. I don't know. It's almost as if she was up to something."

"Some people are just nosy, even coaches." Anna smiles.

"Yeah," I agree. However, it seemed like more than that. I just can't put my finger on it. I had intended to pick her brain about an idea I had but got sidetracked. Oh, well, I'll find my answers another way.

CHAPTER 21
Peyton

I T'S BEEN THREE DAYS SINCE I put my girl on a plane back to Tennessee. Each time, it gets harder and harder to be away from her. My sheets still smell like her, hence the reason I've been staying at my parents' instead of my dorm. Finals are next week anyway, so I'll have to be moving out soon.

Baseball is over, and even though we didn't make the playoffs, it was still one hell of a season, and I pitched a no-hitter with Peyton here to see it. That brings a smile to my face, something that only she seems to be able to do. A call, a text, even a thought of her brightens my day.

Which explains why it's eight at night, and I'm lying here in bed at my parents' place, gripping my phone, waiting for her to call. She had a study group tonight, getting ready for finals next week. I tried to study earlier, but it seems if we're not on a video call while I'm doing it, I can't concentrate.

My phone rings with an incoming video call, and my mood instantly brightens. "Hey."

"Hi. Are you at your parents' place still?" She squints to see the background. I move the phone so she has a better angle.

"I am."

"Tired of the dorms already?"

"Yes, but that's not why I'm here."

"Oh, no. Is something wrong?"

"Yes."

"Tell me." I can see her sit up a little straighter, bracing herself for what I have to say.

"You're not here."

"What?" She tilts her head to the side as a confused expression crosses her face.

"You're not here, but the sheets smell like you. This bed and this room remind me of the weekend we shared, and I can't make myself go back to the dorms."

"You need to marry that one." I hear someone say.

"Where are you?" I ask. Just now realizing I didn't pay close enough attention at the beginning of our call. I was just so happy to see her smiling face.

"I'm at Mom and Dad's."

The next thing I know, her mom's face joins her on the screen. "Hi, Griffin." Larissa waves.

"Hi, Mrs. Monroe," I say, trying to remember my manners. Shit. Her mom heard all of that, and now she's going to hate me.

"Congrats on the win," Larissa says.

"Thank you."

"We watched it on TV," she confesses.

"Wow. Thank you."

"All right, I'm heading to the store. I'll be back." She kisses Peyton on the cheek, and then she's gone.

"She's gone," Peyton tells me.

"I'm sorry. I didn't know she was there."

"It's fine, Griff. She knows."

"She knows what?"

"About our weekend."

"You told her?"

"Yes. We're adults, and well, I'm close to my mom and my sisters."

"And your dad?"

"I'm sure he assumes, but I don't tend to have those kinds of conversations with him. In fact, none of us do. However, he always ends up finding out." She shrugs. "It's usually when he's being all overprotective, and we've had enough, and one of us shouts something that will shock him into silence." She laughs.

"Yeah, let's keep that from happening. I'm trying to get the man to like me, not hate me."

"Oh, he likes you. He's been watching all your televised games. He's also told me several times that you're, and I quote, 'A damn good pitcher,' so I'd say you're winning him over."

"He might think I'm a good pitcher, but I still need him to accept me as your dad, not as a retired baseball player."

"No one needs to accept you but me. And I love you." She smiles. "But he does accept you. He likes you. Trust me. I know my dad. He's just slow to let that out. He wants you to sweat a little. He did the same thing with Cameron and Holden."

"I'm trusting you." I point at the screen.

"You know I've got you."

"I do. So why are you there? I thought you had a study session?"

"We had to end it early. The girl who was leading it, her baby is sick, so she had to go home."

"She's a freshman?"

"She is. She lives locally, and her parents are helping her. She just felt guilty and wanted to be with her son. Not that I blame her. Anyway, I was driving home and decided to stop in and say hi. Dad's at the stadium doing something for Uncle Drew, so it was just Mom and me."

"Wait. Your mom. She's the one that said you should marry me?" I ask, surprised.

"Yep." Her smile is bright.

"Damn."

"I told you."

"I guess we should make that happen then."

"I," She opens her mouth and quickly closes it.

"Cat got your tongue?"

"No, but you do." She chuckles. "Let's live in the same state before we start talking about all that."

"You know we've never talked in detail about when I get drafted, if I get drafted," I amend. "I want you to come with me."

"That's a *ways* away."

"I know what I want, Peyton."

"I'd follow you anywhere," she replies softly.

My heart squeezes. "We've got this, baby. You know that, right?"

She smiles, tears shimmering in her eyes. "Yeah, I know."

We spend the next thirty minutes talking about our days and just getting caught up until Easton comes home.

"Hey, Dad," she says as he bends over and hugs her.

"Missed you, lady," he replies. Then his eyes move to her phone. "Griffin, good game."

"Thank you, sir."

He nods. "Where's Mom?" he asks Peyton.

"She ran to the store."

"Are you staying for dinner?"

"I wasn't planning on it."

"Come on, we never see you."

"Fine." She laughs with a playful roll of her eyes. He kisses the top of her head and walks out of view. "Well, it looks like I'm having dinner here. I'm going to call Karina and see if she wants to come to join us."

"Good idea." I hear Easton say.

"Sounds good. Drive safe going home. Text me when you make it, so I know you're okay."

Her face softens. "I will. Are we still on to study?" she asks.

"Yes."

She nods. "I love you," she says, not hiding the words in front of her father.

It makes me feel ten fucking feet tall. "I love you too." She waves, and then the screen goes black.

I lie here surrounded by her scent for a few more minutes. Finally, my hunger wins out by my growling stomach, and I make my way downstairs. As soon as I hit the bottom step, the smell of whatever is going on in the kitchen hits me, and I quicken my pace.

"Whatever it is, I want a lot of it," I tell my parents, who are cooking together like they always do.

"It's chicken enchiladas," Mom tells me.

I groan. "I'm starving."

"Well, you're just in time to eat," she says, pulling plates out of the cabinet. "How's Peyton today?"

"Good. I just talked to her. She's having dinner with her parents as well."

"You ready for finals next week?"

"I'm getting there. Peyton and I are going to study later."

"How does that work exactly?" Dad asks.

"We just video call each other and study." I shrug.

He nods. "Well, if it works for you."

"It's two birds and one stone. I'd never get to talk to her with baseball and classes if we didn't do it this way. Besides that, she's wicked smart, and we help each other. I've even emailed her my notes, and she's done the same, and we quiz each other. Sometimes, Ollie and Karina join us."

"I can't imagine how hard it is being so far away from her."

"Yeah, I've actually been thinking about that a lot," I confess. I've been trying to find the courage to broach this subject with them.

"Are things not going well?" Dad asks.

"No. They're great. I love her more today than I did yesterday." He nods his understanding.

"Then what's going on?" Mom asks, handing me a plate of enchiladas.

"I hate not being with her. I know we can do this. I know that we can stay together over the distance, but I don't want to."

"Okay?"

"How would you feel if I transferred schools? I was thinking about having Coach Hopkins reach out to the baseball coach at Peyton's school and see if they have room for me." The room is silent. I wipe my sweaty palms on my shorts. They share a look, and then it's my dad who speaks first.

"That's a big move, Griff. That's a big step to take for someone else."

"I'm not taking it for her, Dad. I'm taking it for me. I want to be where she is. It's a good school, and they have a great baseball program."

"You've done your research then?" Mom asks.

"I have. I've been following their team all season. They have a great coaching staff, and it's a D1 school also. It gives me the same opportunities that I have here, but it puts me closer to her."

"What does she think about this?" Dad asks.

"I haven't told her that I've made up my mind. I wanted to talk to the two of you first."

"What about your scholarship?" Mom asks.

"I have my inheritance."

"That's for you to start your life on, Griffin, not pay for college. We have your college fund, but I'm not sure it will cover three years of out-of-state tuition. You do still plan on completing your degree first, right?"

"That's the plan. I'll take out a loan if I have to."

"It sounds like you've made up your mind," Dad says.

"Not entirely, but it's something I've been thinking about a lot. I know we're young, but she's the one. I can feel it."

"And does she feel the same way?" Mom asks.

"Yeah, she does."

"Well, before you take any drastic measures, I think that you should talk to her about this and discuss it. It's important that the two of you are on the same page before this takes place," Dad states.

"Definitely," I agree. "I'm going to think about it some more. I might mention it to Coach Hopkins if the opportunity arises and get his take on it."

"You're a damn good ballplayer, son. I feel confident that no matter which school you attend, scouts will stand up and take notice. I also know that girl loves you, and it's easy to see that you love her. Just remember that communication is the key to a successful relationship. You have to give as much as you take, and I'm damn proud of you for even considering this choice. It shows the man that you are."

"Thanks, Dad," I say, feeling myself start to get choked up.

"I hate the idea of you leaving so soon, but we knew this was going to happen. If you go pro, there is a good chance you're going to have to move anyway."

"*When* he goes pro," Dad corrects her.

"I love you both. Thank you," I tell them.

My parents have always been my biggest supporters, and I'm damn lucky to have them in my life. Knowing that they are behind me on whatever choice I make makes it a little easier to breathe. I'm going to think on this some more, and maybe after finals, track down Coach Hopkins and get his opinion. Sure, he's not going to be happy that I'm leaving, but my heart is no longer in Florida. It lives in Tennessee.

CHAPTER 23
Peyton

Anxiety has my steps faltering as I make my way to my parents' front door. I've made some life decisions that I didn't discuss with them, and I know they're going to be angry. I just needed to do this on my own. I needed to make this choice for me, but that doesn't stop the guilt from weighing heavily on my chest.

Taking a deep breath, I hike my bag up on my shoulder and push open the front door. "Anybody home?" I manage to call out without my voice shaking.

"In here, lady," Dad calls back.

On trembling legs, I make my way to the living room. I take a seat on the couch, my bag and what's inside sitting heavy like a bag of bricks is placed at my feet.

"What a nice surprise," Mom says. "We didn't know you were stopping by today."

"There's something I wanted to talk to you about," I tell them before I lose my nerve.

"Are you pregnant?" Dad asks.

"What? No." I shake my head, giving him an incredulous look.

"Easton!" Mom scolds him.

"What? We have three beautiful daughters." He shrugs like it's a given.

"Ignore your father," Mom tells me. "What's on your mind?"

"Well, I've been thinking a lot, and I've decided on something. Before I tell you what it is, I want to say I'm sorry for not including you in this decision, but I didn't include anyone. I wanted to make this choice for myself and not for anyone else. I didn't want anyone to sway my choice either way, so I kept it to myself."

"Go on," Mom prods gently.

Taking a deep breath, I reach into my bag, pull out the envelope, and hand it to her. My eyes stay glued to her as she pulls out the contents and scans them. Tears well in her eyes, but she's also smiling. That's a good sign, right?

"Oh, honey." She sets the papers next to her on the couch and stands to give me a hug.

"Anyone care to tell me what's going on?" Dad asks.

Mom releases me, then grabs the papers and hands them to Dad. His eyes quickly scan them, and he tosses them on the table. I'm ready for his anger, but instead, he comes to me and pulls Mom and me both into his arms. I feel his lips press to my head, and that causes the dam to break.

"Hey," he says, pulling back. "Why the tears?"

"I thought you were going to be mad at me."

"Is this what you want?"

"Yes."

"Then I'm happy for you. That's all we've ever wanted for our kids is for them to be happy."

"What does Griffin think about all of this?" Mom asks as we all take our seats.

"He doesn't know."

"What?" Dad asks. "You mean to tell me you're uprooting your life to go to school with him, to be closer to him, and he doesn't know?"

"I know Griff. He would have tried to talk me out of it. He would have told me that we can make this work and that it's just a few more years, but I don't want that. I want to be where he is." I pause, taking a deep breath. "He's mentioned moving here before, and I shut him down. He has a full ride, and he's kick-ass with his team. Starting pitcher as a freshman is a huge deal."

"What about your team?" Mom asks.

"The only one I'm close to is Karina, and the others are all catty. They know who our family is and assume that's why I'm on the team. I hate it. The camaraderie that was there in high school just isn't there for me this year."

"We didn't know that," Mom says.

"It's not a big deal. Honestly, had I not met Griff, I would have just let it go, but I did, and that changes things."

"Where are you going to stay?" Mom asks.

"Coach Stone, she's the head coach. She said she'd make sure I could live in a dorm, but I don't know yet. I need to talk to Griffin."

"Are you moving in with him?" Dad asks.

"Maybe?" I shrug. "I know that's not what you want to hear, but if we can make it work, then probably."

Dad picks up the papers again and reads over them. "They gave you a full ride."

"Yes."

"And you already signed with them?"

"Yes."

"Are you happy?"

"Yes."

He studies me. "Then why the tears? Why does it look like someone just kicked your puppy?"

"I don't have a puppy," I counter.

"You know what I mean. What's going on, lady?"

I take a few minutes to get my emotions under control. It's stupid, but it's the last piece of the puzzle that's holding me back. "I feel guilty."

"Guilty?" Mom repeats. "What on earth do you have to feel guilty about?"

"I'm messing up a Monroe family tradition."

"What?" Dad asks.

"You, Mom, Paisley, Parker, and me. We all attended the same college, and now I'm leaving. I feel like I'm abandoning my team." I wipe at my eyes. "You, my family, you're my team, and I feel so guilty for messing up a family tradition and leaving all of you."

My phone rings, and I see Griffin's face. I was supposed to call him an hour ago, but I came here instead. I needed to talk to my parents. "I'm sorry. He's probably worried. I was supposed to call him, but I wanted to come here first."

"Answer it," Dad encourages, which surprises me.

I hit answer and somehow end up putting the call on speaker. "Hey." His deep voice fills the room.

"Hi."

"What's wrong?" he asks.

"What makes you think something's wrong?"

"I can hear it in your voice, baby. What's going on?"

"Nothing. I'm with Mom and Dad. I had to stop by and give them some news."

"What news?"

I look at my mom, and she nods. My gaze moves to my dad, and he does the same. "I needed to tell them about something I did. Something I was worried they would be mad about, but it turns out I was wrong."

"Of course you were. They love you."

My dad smiles at that.

"I know they do, but I was still worried about their reaction. About disappointing them."

"I don't know them well, but from what I do know and from what you've told me about them, that would never happen. Do you want to talk about it? Are you okay?"

"Yeah, I'm okay."

He audibly sighs. "Good. Now, tell me what's got you upset."

"I'm just emotional."

"I hate that I'm not there with you, but they are. They love you. Let them get you through this, whatever it is."

"I want to tell you."

"I'm all ears, baby."

"Are you sitting down?"

"Are you pregnant?" he blurts out, and I feel my face flame. "If you are, we'll figure it out. It's sooner than what I had planned, but I love you, and we can do this. I know we can. I talked to Coach Hopkins earlier. He's going to call the head coach of the boys' team at your school and explain that I need to be in Tennessee and see if they have room for me on their roster."

"You did?"

"I can't live this far away from you. I'm already hoping to go pro, and that's going to have me gone all the time, and yeah." He sighs. "I'm sorry I didn't tell you, but I wanted to see if it was even possible first. But if we're having a baby, that changes things. I'm coming to you no matter what the coach says."

"Griffin." He stops talking. "I'm moving to Florida."

"Wait. What?"

"I signed with Coach Stone earlier this week. It's official. I'm coming to you."

"Peyton, what about the Monroe family going to the same school? That's your family tradition. I can't let you do this. Call her and tell her that you changed your mind."

My mom places her hand over her heart, and that's when I'm reminded that they're hearing this entire conversation. "It's done. Unless you don't want me there?" I add. My heart feels like it could beat out of my chest as I wait for him to speak.

"I want you here." His voice is firm. "I want to be where you are. I don't care if it's here or Tennessee or the North fucking Pole. I'm there if you are," he tells me.

"I think I'll pass on the North Pole."

"When?" he asks.

"I want to spend the rest of the summer here with my family. I know we were going to split our time, but I want to be here. I do need to find a place to stay, and then I'll move before classes start."

"You're going to stay with me."

"You and Oliver were getting a place," I remind him.

"Well, plans change."

"You can't just boot him out of the plan because I decided to move closer to you."

"Damn right I can. He'll understand."

"He can live there too."

"No. No way. I want it to be a place your family will want to come to visit. Not an apartment full of sweaty guys. No. I'll call him and talk to him about it. It will be fine. Sam and Daniel are looking to move out of the dorms too. He can go with them."

"Griffin." I sigh.

"No. I want it to be a home for you. For us. Just until I get drafted. If I get drafted."

"You will."

"If not, I'll be okay. We'll be okay."

"Yeah," I agree. "Listen, I'm still at Mom and Dad's. I'll call you later."

"Okay. I love you."

"I love you too." I end the call and drop my phone into my bag.

Dad sets my signed papers on the table next to him and scoots forward in his chair. His elbows rest on his knees, and his gaze is locked on mine. "He loves you."

I nod. "I love him too."

"Lady, you have nothing to feel guilty about. As parents, we want our children to grow up happy and healthy and find someone to partner this thing we call life with. It makes me happy to know that you and your sisters have found that. I know that I give the men in your lives a hard time, but as your father, I need to know they're worthy of you. That young man of yours just showed me he would move the earth for you if he could."

"I really think he would," I say, wiping the tears from my cheeks.

"And this nonsense about having to go to a certain college, you can let that go. I want you to be happy. I thought that's what you and your sisters wanted. I hope that I didn't make you feel pressured," Mom adds.

"No. You didn't. It was just always unspoken other than comments that all the Monroes went to the same school."

"We're proud of you no matter where you go to school."

"Peyton." Dad waits for me to look at him. "We are always going to be your home team. We're always going to be here for you when you need us, no matter where you live, and no matter how old you get, you're going to be our little girl. However, love goes beyond the team. It's bigger than that, and it sounds to me like your team is growing. You'll have Griffin and his family and his friends. There is a great big world out there, baby girl, and it's waiting for you."

"I love you both. I was so worried," I say as tears fall once more.

"We love you too," Dad says. "I just want you to remember something. Your home team is behind you. We support you, and just know that you always have a place here. If you get to Florida and you want to come home, you call me. I'll make it happen. But I think you're going to be happy there. And," he leans back in his chair, "lucky for you, your mom and I are not only retired, but we also have the means to come and visit you whenever we want. So, you better have that spare bedroom ready." He smiles.

I'm on my feet and headed toward him. He stands, and I crash into him, wrapping my arms around him in a hug. I knew I would be able to convince Mom, but I did not expect this level of understanding or acceptance from my dad. Although, I should have. I saw it with Paisley and Cameron and then again with Parker and Holden. He just wants us to be happy.

Griffin makes me happy.

I spend the next hour with my parents, talking about the move, and with them now on board with my plans, excitement takes over. I'm excited about this next adventure, and even more so, I can be with the man who's stolen my heart.

CHAPTER 24
Griffin

As soon as I hung up the phone with Peyton, I rush downstairs. I officially moved out of the dorms last week, and I'm back home for the summer. Well, that was the plan. Peyton was going to come and visit, and then I was going to do the same. We were going to split our time until classes started again. At least that's what she thought. She didn't know I was going to talk to Coach, and I had no idea she was doing the same.

She's coming here.

I bound into the living room, and my parents look up. "What's got you all happy?" Dad points at my face.

"She's coming here."

"Peyton?" Mom asks.

"Yes."

"I thought you were going there in a few days."

"I am, but she's coming here for good. Well, not for good, but to school. She transferred. Coach Stone signed her. She's transferring." I'm practically bouncing with excitement.

"Did you know?"

"I had no idea. She just told me."

"That changes things," Dad says.

"It does. I know I told you I would help out in the restaurants this summer, but she wants to stay there to be with her family, and I can't fault her for that. I want to spend the entire summer there with her instead of splitting our time."

"Okay," they say at the same time.

"It's that easy?" I ask them.

"You're an adult, Griffin. You can do as you want. You have your own money, and I happen to think that's a good idea. She's leaving her family, and her being close to them until she moves is a good plan."

"Thank you."

"So, where is she staying? Dorms?" Mom asks.

"Hell no," I say. "I want her with me. I need to call Ollie and give him the 'good for me, bad for him' news." I chuckle.

"I'm sure he's going to be fine with it."

"So when you leave in a few days, you'll be gone all summer?" she asks.

"Probably. We do need to find a place to live, so I'm sure we'll come back to take care of that and to see the two of you," I tell them.

"What can we do to help?" Dad asks.

"Bring it in," I say, holding my arms open wide. They both stand and come to me, and I hug them tight. "I love you, guys."

"We love you too."

I stay a little longer before Oliver calls and asks if I want to grab a bite to eat. "That's Ollie. We're going to go eat. Want me to bring something back?" I offer.

"We're good," Mom says. "Your dad and I are meeting up with Steven and Kathy later for dinner."

"Have fun." I wave and turn for the door.

"There's only one thing that puts that goofy-ass grin on your face," Oliver says, pointing at me from across the booth. "How is she?"

"She's fucking perfect," I tell him.

"Wow, okay then." He laughs.

"She's moving here."

"What?" He was in the process of taking a drink of his Mountain Dew but slides it away and waits for my explanation.

I go on to tell him about how she's transferring and moving here after the summer break. "I'm spending the summer there. In Tennessee. When I leave in a few days, I won't be back until school starts."

"So I need to find a new roomie?" He laughs.

"I'm sorry." I do feel bad about it, but not bad enough to change my mind.

"You're fine." He waves me off. "I get it. If I were in your shoes, I'd do the same. Actually, are you driving there?"

"Yeah. I figured it would save on flights, and now, since I'm going to be there all summer, I'll need my Jeep to get around. Maybe I'll find a part-time job or something."

"Are you staying with them?"

"That was the plan. She doesn't know that I'm staying all summer. It's a surprise, but I can't imagine her telling me I can't."

"Yeah, that won't happen." He sits back in the booth and stares down at the table. "You think I could catch a ride with you?" he asks.

"Sure, you going for Karina?"

"Yeah. I've been trying to get her to make this official."

"Long-distance is hard, man, but if it's the right one, it's worth it."

"Maybe I can take the summer to find out?"

"Seriously?" I grin.

"Yeah, as long as they're good with me being there. If not, I can catch a flight home."

"Sounds like a plan to me. A summer with my girl and my best friend. Can't beat it." The server arrives, and we order our pizza. We talk about how so much has changed in the last few months, and I, for one, know I wouldn't change a thing.

"Why are we waiting until this weekend?" he asks as we're finishing up dinner.

I start to reply, but I don't have an answer. "I don't know," I confess.

"I say we pack and get on the road."

"You anxious to see your girl?"

"And make her mine." He nods.

"Let's do it."

"Leave early tomorrow morning?" he asks.

"It's around thirteen hours straight through."

"We can take turns driving and napping. Hit drive-throughs for food."

"I'm down. We'll leave early."

"Done."

My cell rings, and I hit accept on the steering wheel. "Hey, babe," I greet Peyton.

"Hi. What are you doing?"

"Oh, Oliver and I just hit a drive-through for some grub." It's not a lie. We did just hit a drive-through. What I don't tell her is that my GPS says that we're only about an hour from her.

"Nice. Karina just went to pick up Chinese."

"Did you order your sweet-and-sour chicken?" I ask her.

"You know it." I hear her rustling around on the other end of the line. "What did you all get?" She asks.

"Just some burgers and fries." It's not a lie, but I don't want to tell her the name of the restaurant. She might know we don't have them in Florida.

"Well, I'll let you go since you're driving. Call me later."

"Okay. We're going to just drive around for a while and chill."

"I'll be up," she assures me.

"Love you."

"I love you too," she says and ends the call.

"She's going to flip."

"I know. Karina will, too, you know. Peyton told me last night that she's really into you, but long-distance scares her. She's been there as we've navigated it."

"I know, but you two are rock stars. You've made it look easy."

"It's not easy," I assure him. "I miss her every fucking day, but that's over now."

"But worth it, right?"

"So damn worth it."

He moves, adjusting his position. "I'm ready to get there. I know that. Thirteen hours turned into sixteen by the time we get there."

"Yeah, I wasn't expecting a traffic jam, but we're close. Grab a nap. I'll wake you when we're closer."

"No way can I sleep knowing we're almost there. You want me to drive so that you can?" he asks.

"Nah. No sleep for me either." I glance at the dash. "Forty-five more minutes."

We spend the last part of the journey talking about how we'll surprise the girls, and we decide to just knock on the door. We're both too exhausted to put more effort into it, and that's going to be a shock to both of them. It's simple, but it works.

Idle chitchat gets us through the last leg of the trip, and it seems like it takes hours before we're pulling up outside of their apartment building.

"Finally," Oliver says, climbing out of the Jeep.

I grab my phone and keys, and we grab our luggage, which is much more than we would need if we were just staying the week that the girls expect us. Together, we make our way to their door and knock.

I can hear movement inside, and Karina asks, "Who could that be?"

"Probably a delivery with the wrong apartment number," Peyton replies as the door opens.

"Uh, Peyton, I think you need to see this." Karina stands with her mouth hanging open.

"What is it?" I hear my girl as she comes into view. "What? How are you here?" She squeals and launches herself at me. I drop my bags and catch her with ease.

"Missed you," I say, my face buried in her neck.

"Guys, let's bring this inside." Oliver laughs as he steps into the apartment. I lift my head in time to see him bend to kiss Karina on the lips.

Slowly, I lower Peyton to the ground and grab my bags. "We wanted to surprise you."

"Well, you certainly did that. I'm so glad you're here," she says, closing the door behind us. "That's a lot of luggage for a week." She eyes our bags.

"About that." I glance over at Oliver, and he's smiling. "We thought we'd just stay the summer."

"No. Way!"

"Wait." Karina turns to look at Oliver. "You're staying too?" she asks.

"If that's all right."

She launches herself at him, much like Peyton did to me when she opened the door. "That's more than all right."

"Oliver, it's good to see you. Karina, I love you. We're going to bed." Peyton grabs my hand and tugs me to her room, our friends' laughter following us down that hall.

"I should go get my bags."

"No. What you should do is hold me. I've missed you," she says, wrapping her arms around my waist.

"No more," I tell her. "I'm here all summer to spend some time with you and to get to know your family better. Then we move back to Florida for school, and we will come back as much as we can."

"We're really doing this."

"We are." I kick off my shoes, strip out of my T-shirt and shorts, and climb into bed. "I'm exhausted," I tell her.

"Let me change." I watch as she removes her clothes, everything but her panties, and pulls my T-shirt over her head before hitting the light and settling next to me.

"Tell me how your parents took this. I know you said fine, but there had to be more."

"It really was fine. I was worried about breaking the family tradition, but they assured me that it was silly and never meant to be a tradition. It was just something that happened. I told them I felt like I was leaving my team, but not my team... them. They're more of a team than the one I was playing for."

"What did they say to that?"

"Dad gave me this super-sweet speech about how they would always be my home team, but that what we have goes beyond the team I already have. He said I was adding you and your family and friends to my own team, but they would always be there for me. I probably totally botched that, but you get the idea."

"He's a smart man."

"He is."

"I like it, though. The idea that we're making our own team. I think we should wait until we're graduated to start adding players, but we can practice," I tell her, sliding my hand under her shirt.

"I thought you were exhausted?"

"I am, but I'll never be too tired for you."

"Sleep. We have all summer to practice."

"No, baby. We have the rest of our lives to make it happen," I say, covering a yawn. She settles on my chest, our arms wrapped around each other, and I drift off to the best night's sleep I've had since the last time I held her in my arms.

CHAPTER 25
Peyton

IT'S HARD TO BELIEVE THAT summer is coming to an end. Today, my family is getting together at my parents' place for a going away party. We don't leave for a few more days, but Cameron and Holden had a rare day off, and we like to take advantage when that happens.

"You ready?" Griffin asks. "I told your dad we would be there early to fire up the grill."

That's a new development too. Griffin was determined to show my family that he was in this. That sure, we might be young, but we know what we want. He also wanted to prove that he could play on team Monroe. I'm not sure exactly how it happened, but he and my dad bonded over grilling steaks, and it's been a bromance ever since. Not that I'm complaining. My dad's a big ole softy at heart, but I'm glad he and Griffin are getting along so well.

"I'm ready."

"Ollie and Karina are going to meet us there later. They went to see her grandma in the nursing home," he tells me.

"Oh, I didn't realize they weren't home."

"They left while you were in the shower."

"Sounds good. I'm ready to go." He takes my hand and leads me to his Jeep. We've just turned on my parents' road when Karina calls. "Hey, are you all still stopping at Mom and Dad's?"

"We are." She sounds happy. Excited even.

"What's up?" I ask her.

"Nothing. Just been a good day. I was calling to tell you that we're on our way."

"Okay, well, we just pulled in."

"See you soon."

"She's extra happy today," I tell Griffin, dropping my phone into the cup holder.

"Is she?" he asks.

I turn to look at him. "You know something."

"Dammit." He laughs. "Okay, I know something, but I told her I wouldn't tell, and I found out by accident."

"Is it a good something?"

"Yes."

"Okay then. I'll let you off the hook." I turn to reach for the handle and see a car I don't recognize in the driveway. "Do you know who that is?" I ask him.

"No. Maybe one of the guys bought a new car."

"Maybe," I say, not really thinking that, but I could be wrong. Instead of going into the house, we walk around back to the patio, where we know everyone will be. What we find has me stopping in my tracks.

Griffin bumps into me, his hands going to my hips to keep me from falling over. "Babe?"

I point at the back patio.

"Holy shit." He kisses my cheek and takes off, running toward his parents, who are standing there, talking to mine. I rush after him and hug them once Griffin is through.

"What are you guys doing here?"

"Easton said you've been boasting about your grilling skills, and I had to let him know who the true grill master is in the Anthony family," Gary jokes.

"No. For real. What are you doing here? Not that I'm upset, I'm happy to see you, but what are you doing here?" he asks again.

"Larissa and I are friends on social media," Anna explains. "She reached out to us and told us about the party, and we thought it was a good time for all of us to meet."

"We're coming home in a few days."

"We know that, but we missed both of you and wanted to meet her family," Dad says.

"It's more than that. I felt it was important for them to know that Peyton is going to have a huge support system in Florida. We can't replace them, but we can help fill the void." My mom looks at Larissa, and she smiles at her before coming closer and wrapping my mom in a hug.

Griffin stays at the grill with his dad and mine while I go to say hi to my sisters and steal baby Penelope from her daddy.

"Oh no, you don't," Cameron warns me. "All of you women are baby hogs." He points at Holden. "And you, get your own," he says.

"Come on, Cam. I leave in a few days, and I'm going to miss you so much. Hand her over."

"Fine," he grumbles. He kisses his daughter's head and stands, giving me his chair, before placing her in my arms. "Hold her head," he tells me.

"I got it." I laugh, as do my sisters.

I love on my new baby niece and just take it all in. Mom and Anna are sitting under a shade tree talking as if they've known each other for years. Holden, Cameron, and Oliver are tossing a football, much to their dismay, with Jett. Karina, Paisley, Parker, and I are all just sitting around the patio table, talking and laughing, while Dad, Gary, and Griffin are manning the grill.

"You okay over there?" Paisley asks.

"I'm more than okay. It feels like it's taken years to get to this moment, but I wouldn't change it. Not for anything." My sisters nod, and I know they understand what I'm saying.

"How about some more news?" Karina asks.

"Yes. You've been holding out on me. Griffin wouldn't even tell me."

"Yeah, he kind of heard us talking and found out. I made him promise not to tell you until I talked to my parents."

"What's going on?" She's smiling, so it has to be good news.

"Well, you know that Oliver and I made things official."

"That was weeks ago."

She nods. "Yeah, and I don't want to do what you and Griffin did. I don't know that I'm strong enough to be away from him for that long, so I'm moving too."

"What did you just say? I thought I heard you say you were moving?"

"You heard me." She smiles. "I'm moving to Florida with you. Oliver and I rented a place in the same complex as you and Griffin."

"Explain." It's not that I'm not happy. Of course, I am, but I need to know how this happened.

"I'm not feeling softball. I loved it in high school, but college is altogether different. I applied to a new school, but it's close by, and I changed my major."

"What?"

"I want to be a pediatric nurse. I've been thinking about it for a while and decided it was time for a change. Our school doesn't have a nursing program, but there is one about fifteen miles from the new apartment. They accepted me. It's a four-year bachelor's program."

"I'm thrilled for you," I tell her. "Why didn't you tell me?"

"I wasn't sure it was all going to work out. And I didn't want you to think that I was following you. I mean, I am, and I love you, but this is something I've wanted, and well, Oliver is just a bonus in all of this."

"Wow."

"Good for you," Paisley tells her.

"I'm proud of you for chasing your dreams," Parker adds.

"It's a win-win if you think about it. I get to do something I love. I get to live next to my best friend and be with the man I love."

"That's me if you didn't know," Oliver says, stepping up behind her and placing his hands on her shoulders.

"I got that." I laugh at him.

"Did she finally tell you?" Griffin asks. He leans over my chair and offers Penelope his finger.

"She did."

"Good surprise?" he asks.

"The best."

"Good, now hand over the baby."

"What? No. We're leaving soon."

"Exactly. I should get a turn too." He stands and nods toward my niece, and I relent, handing her over.

I swear there is an audible sigh at the table as all four of us watch as he cradles her in his arms and smiles down at her. "We're getting one of these, Peyton. Maybe a dozen," he tells me.

"Let's start with one in a few years and see how it goes."

"I was an only child. I want our kids to have siblings like you do."

"This doesn't have to be decided now," I tell him.

"No, I guess not. But I have witnesses." He points at my sisters, Karina, and Oliver. "Take notes in case she argues in a few years. She agreed to it."

"Anthony, give me my daughter."

"Fine," Griffin grumbles good-naturedly and hands her back to her daddy.

"Great. Now we'll never get her back," I whine.

"How about you stop by the house in the next couple of days? Cam will be back on the road for a three-day stretch, and you can soak up all the cuddles you can stand," Paisley offers.

I look up at Griffin, and he's already nodding. "Consider it done."

"Let's eat!" Dad calls out.

The rest of the day is filled with love, laughter, good food, and even better company. In no way would I have ever imagined that meeting a guy on spring break would lead to this. I had no way of knowing how he would change my life for the better.

My dad was right. This love and the love that surrounds us is beyond the team. I can't wait to see what happens next.

EPILOGUE

Griffin

Four Years Later

THIS IS IT. THE FINAL game of the World Series. Our starting pitcher tore his rotator cuff and needed surgery three months into the season, and that put me on the mound. This is my first season in the majors, and it's been an honor to be here. I stare up at the crowd, and I know my friends and family are here.

I know that my wife is sitting with my parents and hers, as well as her sisters, and nieces and nephews. I also know that her best friend and her baby girl, Olivia, are sitting next to her.

Life has a funny way of working out, and I was drafted to the Tennessee Blaze. I had other offers, some more money, but this is where we wanted to be. I wanted my wife to have her family close while I'm on the road. We want a big family, and she needs that support system.

Oliver was drafted as well, but he's on the farm team. He's in the stands with his wife and their baby girl. Olivia just turned a year old, and she's the cutest baby. I've been telling my wife, yes, wife. I married her the week after we graduated from college. Anyway, I've been telling my wife that we need to start our family. Don't get me wrong, we're having the time of our lives practicing, but I'm ready for what comes next. I'm ready for anything life tosses our way as long as she's right by my side.

Shaking out of my thoughts, I get my head back in the game. Two outs, and the bases are loaded. We're up by three, but if they get this hit, that could change the game, as well as the title of World Series winners could be over.

I wind up the pitch and let it fly.

"Strike!" the umpire calls out.

"Two more," I mutter to myself.

Taking my time, I pull in a deep breath, wind up the pitch, and let it fly.

"Strike two!"

"Fuck." I take off my glove and place it under my arm, then remove my hat from my head and run my fingers through my hair. One more. One more strike, and we win. The Blaze takes the World Series win.

Sliding back into my glove, I wind up the pitch and give it all that I've got. It feels like it takes an eternity for the ball to make it to the plate, but I know that's not true. I've been throwing in the 90 miles per hour range. When the ball gets there, the batter swings and misses.

He fucking misses.

The crowd goes wild, and my teammates tackle me.

"Fuck, yeah!" Holden lifts me in the air and shakes me.

"My man!" Cameron shouts, pulling me into a hug as soon as Holden drops me to my feet.

They're my brothers. Not just by marriage, but on the field and in life. I look up to the stands where I know our family sits, and I need to get to her. I need Peyton. I have a lump in the back of my throat the size of Texas, and hot tears are pricking my eyes. She is my biggest cheerleader, my biggest supporter, and I need her. Right here. Right now. This moment belongs to my team, it belongs to me, and it belongs to us and our family. I scan the crowd, and I see her. She's holding Olivia in her arms, and she's smiling widely, and I can't see them, but I know tears are racing down her cheeks.

I ignore the reporters and I ignore the fans, and even my teammates as I jog toward her. I need my wife.

EPILOGUE

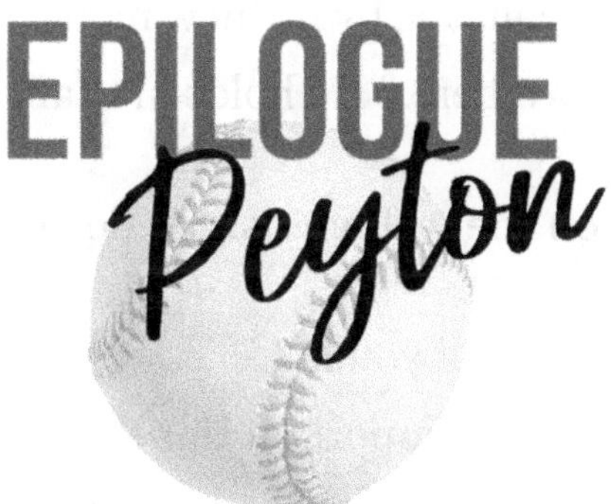

H

E DID IT. MY HEART hammers in my chest, and I choke back the sob that's threatening to break free. My husband and my brothers-in-law are World Series champions. I hold baby Olivia closer, and she places her little arms around my neck.

Around me, our friends and family are cheering for our team and the three men who we love dearly. I feel an arm wrap around me, and I turn to see my mother-in-law, Anna.

"He did it," she smiles.

"He did."

She and Gary flew in a couple of days ago, and it's been great to be able to catch up with them. They're talking about moving here to be closer to us. Especially when we finally decide to give them grandchildren. Their words, not mine.

"Look." Anna points at the field, and I spot him immediately as he stalks his way to where we're sitting.

Carefully, I hand Olivia off to her momma and start to descend the stairs. I hold the railing with each step. My smile is wide, and my heart is so full for him and the entire Blaze team.

"Mrs. Anthony," Griffin smiles up at me.

"Mr. Anthony." We've been married a year, and it still gives me a thrill when he calls me by my new name.

"Get your ass down here." He holds his hands up to reach for me.

Carefully, I sit on the wall and smile down at him. "Are you going to catch me?"

"You know I'd never let you fall."

"I know, but it's really important this time."

He tilts his head to the side, and I can see the moment he understands what I'm trying to tell him. "Yeah?" he asks.

I nod.

"I won't let you fall." There is so much conviction in his voice and love in his eyes that I know he's right.

I take the leap, and he catches me easily. He doesn't let me go, but instead maneuvers so that my legs are wrapped around his waist and my arms around his neck.

"We're having a baby?" he asks.

I nod. I can't seem to find my voice from the awe in his.

"Just when I thought this day couldn't be any better." His lips press against mine, and everything around us fades away. It's just my husband and me standing on the field, holding each other celebrating both a personal and a professional win.

"We're starting our team," I say once I find my voice.

"Nah, baby, this goes beyond the team." He smiles. "This is our family, our life, and our future. I love you, Mrs. Anthony."

"I love you too."

BONUS SCENE
Easton

Eleven Years Later

I'M SITTING IN THE BACKYARD holding my youngest granddaughter, Kinzie, in my arms. She's four, and just like the rest of her cousins, she has me wrapped around her little finger. I came out here to rock her to sleep under the shade tree away from the crowd. She's been asleep for a while, but I can't seem to find the will to stand and take her inside just yet.

Instead, I'm sitting here watching my family. My wife is standing with our grandson Jett. Today is his eighteenth birthday. He's over a head taller than her, but he's a big teddy bear just like his daddy. At least when it comes to the women in the family: his grandma, his mom, his aunts, his sister, and his cousins. As the eldest, he takes his responsibility seriously, and I'd love to say that's my influence, but I know it's from his dad, Cameron. He's a good man.

I hear a squeal of laughter, and my eyes trail until I find the source. Holden and Parker are in the pool. Their twins, Sara and Sean, are on their shoulders playing a game of chicken. Their eldest, Mitchell, sits on the edge of the pool, cheering them on.

Jett comes out of nowhere with his sister, Penelope, thrown over his shoulder and jumps into the pool. The splash is huge, and the laughter that follows fills my heart.

My gaze travels until I find Peyton and Griffin. They're sitting on a lounge chair with their son, Hank, sitting next to them. His hands are moving as he tells them a story that has them both smiling.

Kinzie squirms and squints open her eyes. "Pappa?"

"Yeah, baby?"

"I love you."

"I love you too," I tell her.

"I'm thirsty."

"Well, let's see what we can do about that." I stand and head toward the rest of our family.

Griffin sees me. He leans over and kisses Peyton softly, rubs his hand through Hank's hair, then makes his way toward me. "Baby girl, you want to give Pappa a break?" he asks his daughter.

"I'm thirsty, Daddy."

"Well, let's fix that."

She holds her arms out for him, and he takes her easily, snuggling her close.

I don't try to hide my smile as he walks away to do her bidding. It's not lost on me that his reply was the same as mine. As bad as I first hated to admit it, my daughters all married men who worship them, like I do their mother.

Speaking of, my wife is headed my way. I open my arms wide for her, and she walks right into them, resting her head on my chest where she belongs.

"I never could have imagined this, Easton. All those years ago, when you came into my work, I never would have guessed we would end up here."

"We've made a wonderful life and a beautiful family."

"Thank you for this life."

"I should be thanking you. You took a chance on me. You and Paisley, you made me fall in love with you, and I've never looked back."

"I never thought I would find a man to love us both, to love her like you do."

"I never had a chance." I chuckle. "You both stole my heart, and here we are. Three daughters who are smart, intelligent women. They've found men who love them like they deserve to be loved, and they've given us all of these extra hearts to love."

"I always thought a life like this was out of reach."

"I told you. Beyond the bases, baby."

I cannot thank you enough for taking the time to read
Beyond the Team.
If you're looking for your next read, try **Play by Play** *it's a free prequel to the Riggins Brothers Series.*

Other titles in the **Out of Reach Series:**

Beyond the Bases

Beyond the Game

Beyond the Play

Beyond the Team

Never miss a new release:
Newsletter Sign-up

Be the first to hear about free content, new releases, cover reveals, sales, and more. kayleeryan.com/subscribe/

Discover more about Kaylee's books
kayleeryan.com/all-books/

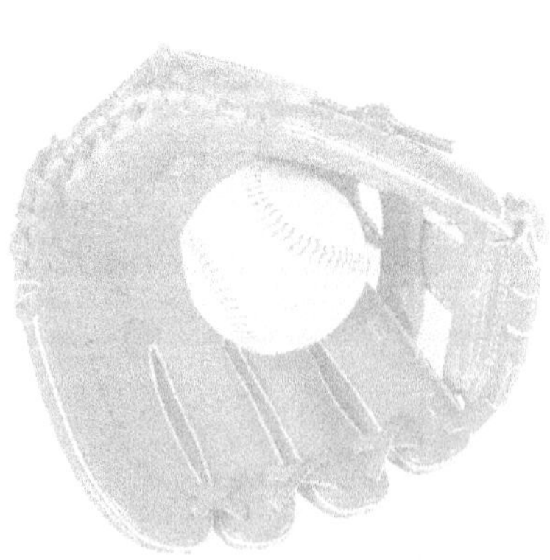

CONTACT
Kaylee Ryan

Facebook:

bit.ly/2C5DgdF

Reader Group:

bit.ly/2O0yWDx

Goodreads:

bit.ly/2HodJvx

BookBub:

bit.ly/2KulVvH

Website:

kayleeryan.com/

ALSO BY Kaylee Ryan

With You Series:
Anywhere with You | More with You | Everything with You

Soul Serenade Series:
Emphatic | Assured | Definite | Insistent

Southern Heart Series:
Southern Pleasure | Southern Desire
Southern Attraction | Southern Devotion

Unexpected Arrivals Series
Unexpected Reality |Unexpected Fight | Unexpected Fall
Unexpected Bond | Unexpected Odds

Riggins Brothers Series:
Play by Play | Layer by Layer | Piece by Piece
Kiss by Kiss | Touch by Touch | Beat by Beat

Entangled Hearts Duet:
Agony | Bliss

Cocky Hero Club:
Lucky Bastard

ACKNOWLEDGMENTS

I never planned to turn Beyond the Bases into a series. It started out as a novella for an Amazon Kindle World. The program was discontinued before the novella was released. So, I added some content and put it out into the universe. The response from readers was overwhelming. You loved Easton and Larissa, and the girls too. I can't tell you how many messages and emails I've received asking for the daughters to have their own stories. Hence, the Out of Reach Series was born. Thank you so very much for loving my words. I love what I do, and you, my readers, make it easy. Thank you for devouring my words and then shouting about them from the rooftops. Your never-ending support is unparalleled.

To my family: My support system. I could not do this without you in my corner. Thank you for taking this wild ride with me. I love you.

Wander Aguiar: Thank you for another incredible image. It's always a pleasure working with you and Andrey.

Sommer Stein: Thank you for making each cover fit the Out of Reach branding. I love them all!

Lacey Black: My dear friend. Thank you for always being there with life and work. I value our friendship and our working relationship more than you will ever know. I can't wait to see what our co-writing journey takes us.

My beta team: Jamie, Stacy, Lauren, Erica, and Franci, I would be lost without you. You read my words as much as I do, and I can't tell you what your input and all the time you give means to me. Countless messages and bouncing ideas, you ladies keep me sane with the characters are being anything but. Thank you from the bottom of my heart for taking this wild ride with me.

Give Me Books: With every release, your team works diligently to get my book in the hands of bloggers. I cannot tell you how thankful I am for your services.

Tempting Illustrations: Thank you for everything. I would be lost without you.

Julie Deaton: Thank you for giving this book a set of fresh final eyes.

Jenny Sims: Thank you for helping polish this book to be the best that it can be.

Becky Johnson: I could not do this without you. Thank you for pushing me and making me work for it.

Brittany Holland: Thank you for your assistance with the blurb. You saved me!

Chasidy Renee: Thank you for everything you do. How did I survive without you before now?

Erica Caudill & Kaitie Reister: Thank you both for your baseball expertise. You helped me so much with this series.

Bloggers: Thank you, it doesn't seem like enough. You don't get paid to do what you do. It's the kindness of your heart and your love of reading that fuels you. Without you, without your pages, your voice, your reviews, spreading the word, it would be so much harder, if not impossible, to get my words in the reader's hands. I can't tell you how much your never-ending support means to me. Thank you for being you. Thank you for all that you do.

To my reader group, Kaylee's Crew: You are my people. I love all of the messages and emails you send me. I love the little book community we've created. You are my family. Thank you for all of your love and support, not just with books but with life. No matter what I decide to write, you are there, ready to consume every word. Thank you for being the amazing group of people that you are.

With Love,

Kaylee Ryan
AUTHOR